Agatha Christie is known throughout the world as the Queen of Crime. She is the most widely published author of all time and in any language, outsold only by the Bible and Shakespeare. She is the author of 80 crime novels and short story collections, 19 plays, and six novels written under the name of Mary Westmacott.

Agatha Christie's first novel, *The Mysterious Affair at Styles*, was written towards the end of the First World War, in which she served as a VAD. In it she created Hercule Poirot, the little Belgian detective who was destined to become the most popular detective in crime fiction since Sherlock Holmes.

Agatha Christie was made a Dame in 1971. She died in 1976.

MRS McGINTY'S DEAD

Mrs McGinty dies from a brutal blow to the back of her head. Suspicion falls immediately on her shifty lodger, James Bentley, whose clothes reveal traces of the victim's blood and hair. Yet something is amiss: Bentley simply doesn't seem like a murderer! Could the answer lie in an article clipped from a newspaper just days before the death? With a desperate killer still free, Hercule Poirot will have to stay alive long enough to find out . . .

Agatha Christie

AGATHA CHRISTIE

◆

MRS McGINTY'S DEAD

Complete and Unabridged

ULVERSCROFT
Leicester

First published in Great Britain in 1952 by
Collins
London

First Large Print Edition
published 2011
by arrangement with
HarperCollins*Publishers*
London

British Library CIP Data

Christie, Agatha, *1890 – 1976.*
  Mrs McGinty's dead.
  1. Poirot, Hercule (Fictitious character)- -Fiction.
  2. Private investigators- -Belgium- -Fiction.
  3. Detective and mystery stories. 4. Large type books.
  I. Title
  823.9′12–dc22

ISBN 978–1–44480–268–9

Published by
F. A. Thorpe (Publishing)
Anstey, Leicestershire

To Peter Saunders
in gratitude for his kindness
to authors

1

Hercule Poirot came out of the *Vieille Grand'mère* restaurant into Soho. He turned up the collar of his overcoat through prudence, rather than necessity, since the night was not cold. 'But at my age, one takes no risks,' Poirot was wont to declare.

His eyes held a reflective sleepy pleasure. The *Escargots de la Vieille Grand'mère* had been delicious. A real find, this dingy little restaurant. Meditatively, like a well fed dog, Hercule Poirot curled his tongue round his lips. Drawing his handkerchief from his pocket, he dabbed his luxuriant moustaches.

Yes, he had dined well . . . And now what?

A taxi, passing him, slowed down invitingly. Poirot hesitated for a moment, but made no sign. Why take a taxi? He would in any case reach home too early to go to bed.

'Alas,' murmured Poirot to his moustaches, 'that one can only eat three times a day . . . '

For afternoon tea was a meal to which he had never become acclimatized. 'If one partakes of the five o'clock, one does not,' he explained, 'approach the dinner with the proper quality of expectant gastric juices. And the dinner, let us remember, is the supreme meal of the day!'

Not for him, either, the mid-morning coffee. No, chocolate and *croissants* for breakfast, *Déjeuner* at twelve-thirty if possible but certainly not later than one o'clock, and finally the climax: *Le Dîner!*

These were the peak periods of Hercule Poirot's day. Always a man who had taken his stomach seriously, he was reaping his reward in old age. Eating was now not only a physical pleasure, it was also an intellectual research. For in between meals he spent quite a lot of time searching out and marking down possible sources of new and delicious food. *La Vieille Grand'mère* was the result of one of these quests and *La Vieille Grand'mère* had just received the seal of Hercule Poirot's gastronomic approval.

But now, unfortunately, there was the evening to put in.

Hercule Poirot sighed.

'If only,' he thought, '*ce cher Hastings* were available . . . '

He dwelt with pleasure on his remembrances of his old friend.

'My first friend in this country — and still to me the dearest friend I have. True, often and often did he enrage me. But do I remember that now? No. I remember only his

2

incredulous wonder, his open-mouthed appreciation of my talents — the ease with which I misled him without uttering an untrue word, his bafflement, his stupendous astonishment when he at last perceived the truth that had been clear to me all along. *Ce cher, cher ami!* It is my weakness, it has always been my weakness, to desire to show off. That weakness, Hastings could never understand. But indeed it is very necessary for a man of my abilities to admire himself — and for that one needs stimulation from outside. I cannot, truly I cannot, sit in a chair all day reflecting how truly admirable I am. One needs the human touch. One needs — as they say nowadays — the *stooge.*'

Hercule Poirot sighed. He turned into Shaftesbury Avenue.

Should he cross it and go on to Leicester Square and spend the evening at a cinema? Frowning slightly, he shook his head. The cinema, more often than not, enraged him by the looseness of its plots — the lack of logical continuity in the argument — even the photography which, raved over by some, to Hercule Poirot seemed often no more than the portrayal of scenes and objects so as to make them appear totally different from what they were in reality.

Everything, Hercule Poirot decided, was

too artistic nowadays. Nowhere was there the love of order and method that he himself prized so highly. And seldom was there any appreciation of subtlety. Scenes of violence and crude brutality were the fashion, and as a former police officer, Poirot was bored by brutality. In his early days, he had seen plenty of crude brutality. It had been more the rule than the exception. He found it fatiguing, and unintelligent.

'The truth is,' Poirot reflected as he turned his steps homeward, 'I am not in tune with the modern world. And I am, in a superior way, a slave as other men are slaves. My work has enslaved me just as their work enslaves them. When the hour of leisure arrives, they have nothing with which to fill their leisure. The retired financier takes up golf, the little merchant puts bulbs in his garden, me, I eat. But there it is, I come round to it again. *One can only eat three times a day.* And in between are the gaps.'

He passed a newspaper-seller and scanned the bill.

'Result of McGinty Trial. Verdict.'

It stirred no interest in him. He recalled vaguely a small paragraph in the papers. It had not been an interesting murder. Some wretched old woman knocked on the head for a few pounds. All part of the senseless crude

4

brutality of these days.

Poirot turned into the courtyard of his block of flats. As always his heart swelled in approval. He was proud of his home. A splendid symmetrical building. The lift took him up to the third floor where he had a large luxury flat with impeccable chromium fittings, square armchairs, and severely rectangular ornaments. There could truly be said not to be a curve in the place.

As he opened the door with his latchkey and stepped into the square, white lobby, his manservant, George, stepped softly to meet him.

'Good evening, sir. There is a — gentleman waiting to see you.'

He relieved Poirot deftly of his overcoat.

'Indeed?' Poirot was aware of that very slight pause before the word *gentleman*. As a social snob, George was an expert.

'What is his name?'

'A Mr Spence, sir.'

'Spence.' The name, for the moment, meant nothing to Poirot. Yet he knew that it should do so.

Pausing for a moment before the mirror to adjust his moustaches to a state of perfection, Poirot opened the door of the sitting-room and entered. The man sitting in one of the big square armchairs got up.

'Hallo, M. Poirot, hope you remember me. It's a long time . . . Superintendent Spence.'

'But of course.' Poirot shook him warmly by the hand.

Superintendent Spence of the Kilchester Police. A very interesting case that had been . . . As Spence had said, a long time ago now . . .

Poirot pressed his guest with refreshments. A *grenadine? Crème de Menthe? Benedictine? Crème de Cacao?* . . .

At this moment George entered with a tray on which was a whisky bottle and a siphon. 'Or beer if you prefer it, sir?' he murmured to the visitor.

Superintendent Spence's large red face lightened.

'Beer for me,' he said.

Poirot was left to wonder once more at the accomplishments of George. He himself had had no idea that there was beer in the flat and it seemed incomprehensible to him that it could be preferred to a sweet liqueur.

When Spence had his foaming tankard, Poirot poured himself out a tiny glass of gleaming green *Crème de Menthe*.

'But it is charming of you to look me up,' he said. 'Charming. You have come up from — ?'

'Kilchester. I'll be retired in about six

months. Actually, I was due for retirement eighteen months ago. They asked me to stop on and I did.'

'You were wise,' said Poirot with feeling. 'You were very wise . . . '

'Was I? I wonder. I'm not so sure.'

'Yes, yes, you were wise,' Poirot insisted. 'The long hours of *ennui*, you have no conception of them.'

'Oh, I'll have plenty to do when I retire. Moved into a new house last year, we did. Quite a bit of garden and shamefully neglected. I haven't been able to get down to it properly yet.'

'Ah yes, you are one of those who garden. Me, once I decided to live in the country and grow vegetable marrows. It did not succeed. I have not the temperament.'

'You should have seen one of my marrows last year,' said Spence with enthusiasm. 'Colossal! And my roses. I'm keen on roses. I'm going to have — '

He broke off.

'That's not what I came to talk about.'

'No, no, you came to see an old acquaintance — it was kind. I appreciate it.'

'There's more to it than that, I'm afraid, M. Poirot. I'll be honest. I want something.'

Poirot murmured delicately:

'There is a mortgage, possibly, on your

house? You would like a loan — '

Spence interrupted in a horrified voice:

'Oh, good Lord, it's not *money*! Nothing of that kind.'

Poirot waved his hands in graceful apology.

'I demand your pardon.'

'I'll tell you straight out — it's damned cheek what I've come for. If you send me away with a flea in my ear I shan't be surprised.'

'There will be no flea,' said Poirot. 'But continue.'

'It's the McGinty case. You've read about it, perhaps?'

Poirot shook his head.

'Not with attention. Mrs McGinty — an old woman in a shop or a house. She is dead, yes. How did she die?'

Spence stared at him.

'Lord!' he said. 'That takes me back. Extraordinary. And I never thought of it until now.'

'I beg your pardon?'

'Nothing. Just a game. Child's game. We used to play it when we were kids. A lot of us in a row. Question and answer all down the line. '*Mrs McGinty's dead!*' '*How did she die?*' '*Down on one knee just like I.*' And then the next question, '*Mrs McGinty's dead.*' '*How did she die?*' '*Holding her hand*

8

out just *like* I.' And there we'd be, all kneeling and our right arms held out stiff. And then you *got* it! *'Mrs McGinty's dead.'* *'How did she die?'* *'Like THIS!'* Smack, the top of the row would fall sideways and down we all went like a pack of ninepins!' Spence laughed uproariously at the remembrance. 'Takes me back, it does!'

Poirot waited politely. This was one of the moments when, even after half a lifetime in the country, he found the English incomprehensible. He himself had played at *Cache Cache* in his childhood, but he felt no desire to talk about it or even to think about it.

When Spence had overcome his own amusement, Poirot repeated with some slight weariness, 'How *did* she die?'

The laughter was wiped off Spence's face. He was suddenly himself again.

'She was hit on the back of her head with some sharp, heavy implement. Her savings, about thirty pounds in cash, were taken after her room had been ransacked. She lived alone in a small cottage except for a lodger. Man of the name of Bentley. James Bentley.'

'Ah yes, Bentley.'

'The place wasn't broken into. No signs of any tampering with the windows or locks. Bentley was hard up, had lost his job, and owed two months' rent. The money was

9

found hidden under a loose stone at the back of the cottage. Bentley's coat sleeve had blood on it and hair — same blood group and the right hair. According to his first statement he was never near the body — so it couldn't have come there by accident.'

'Who found her?'

'The baker called with bread. It was the day he got paid. James Bentley opened the door to him and said he'd knocked at Mrs McGinty's bedroom door, but couldn't get an answer. The baker suggested she might have been taken bad. They got the woman from next door to go up and see. Mrs McGinty wasn't in the bedroom, and hadn't slept in the bed, but the room had been ransacked and the floorboards had been prised up. Then they thought of looking in the parlour. She was there, lying on the floor, and the neighbour fairly screamed her head off. Then they got the police, of course.'

'And Bentley was eventually arrested and tried?'

'Yes. The case came on at the Assizes. Yesterday. Open and shut case. The jury were only out twenty minutes this morning. Verdict: Guilty. Condemned to death.'

Poirot nodded.

'And then, after the verdict, you got in a

train and came to London and came here to see me. Why?'

Superintendent Spence was looking into his beer glass. He ran his finger slowly round and round the rim.

'Because,' he said, 'I don't think he did it . . .'

2

There was a moment or two of silence.

'You came to me — '

Poirot did not finish the sentence.

Superintendent Spence looked up. The colour in his face was deeper than it had been. It was a typical countryman's face, unexpressive, self-contained, with shrewd but honest eyes. It was the face of a man with definite standards who would never be bothered by doubts of himself or by doubts of what constituted right and wrong.

'I've been a long time in the Force,' he said. 'I've had a good deal of experience of this, that and the other. I can judge a man as well as any other could do. I've had cases of murder during my service — some of them straightforward enough, some of them not so straightforward. One case *you* know of, M. Poirot — '

Poirot nodded.

'Tricky, that was. But for you, we mightn't have seen clear. But we did see clear — and there wasn't any doubt. The same with the others you don't know about. There was Whistler, he got his — *and* deserved it. There were those chaps who shot old Guterman. There was Verall and his arsenic. Tranter got off — but he did it all right. Mrs Courtland — she was lucky — her husband was a nasty perverted bit of work, and the jury acquitted her accordingly. Not justice — just sentiment. You've got to allow for that happening now and again. Sometimes there isn't enough evidence — sometimes there's sentiment, sometimes a murderer manages to put it across the jury — that last doesn't happen often, but it can happen. Sometimes it's a clever bit of work by defending counsel — or a prosecuting counsel takes the wrong tack. Oh yes, I've seen a lot of things like that. But — but — '

Spence wagged a heavy forefinger.

'I haven't seen — not in *my* experience — an innocent man hanged for something he didn't do. It's a thing, M. Poirot, that I don't *want* to see.

'Not,' added Spence, 'in *this* country!'

Poirot gazed back at him.

'And you think you are going to see it now. But why — '

Spence interrupted him.

'I know some of the things you're going to say. I'll answer them without you having to ask them. I was put on this case. I was put on to get evidence of what happened. I went into the whole business very carefully. I got the facts, all the facts I could. All those facts pointed one way — pointed to one person. When I'd got all the facts I took them to my superior officer. After that it was out of my hands. The case went to the Public Prosecutor and it was up to him. He decided to prosecute — he couldn't have done anything else — not on the evidence. And so James Bentley was arrested and committed for trial, and was duly tried and has been found guilty. They couldn't have found him anything else, not on the evidence. And evidence is what a jury have to consider. Didn't have any qualms about it either, I should say. No, I should say they were all quite satisfied he *was* guilty.'

'But you — are not?'

'No.'

'Why?'

Superintendent Spence sighed. He rubbed his chin thoughtfully with his big hand.

'I don't know. What I mean is, I can't give a reason — a concrete reason. To the jury I dare say he looked like a murderer — to me he didn't — and I know a lot more about murderers than they do.'

'Yes, yes, you are an expert.'

'For one thing, you know, he wasn't *cocky*. Not cocky at all. And in my experience they usually are. Always so damned pleased with themselves. Always think they're stringing you along. Always sure they've been so clever about the whole thing. And even when they're in the dock and must know they're for it, they're still in a queer sort of way getting a kick out of it all. They're in the limelight. They're the central figure. Playing the star part — perhaps for the first time in their lives. They're — well — you know — *cocky!*'

Spence brought out the word with an air of finality.

'You'll understand what I mean by that, M. Poirot.'

'I understand very well. And this James Bentley — he was not like that?'

'No. He was — well, just scared stiff. Scared stiff from the start. And to some people that would square in with his being guilty. But not to me.'

'No, I agree with you. What is he like, this James Bentley?'

'Thirty-three, medium height, sallow complexion, wears glasses — '

Poirot arrested the flow.

'No, I do not mean his physical characteristics. What sort of a personality?'

'Oh — that.' Superintendent Spence considered. 'Unprepossessing sort of fellow. Nervous manner. Can't look you straight in the face. Has a sly sideways way of peering at you. Worst possible sort of manner for a jury. Sometimes cringing and sometimes truculent. Blusters in an inefficient kind of way.'

He paused and added in a conversational tone:

'Really a shy kind of chap. Had a cousin rather like that. If anything's awkward they go and tell some silly lie that hasn't a chance of being believed.'

'He does not sound attractive, your James Bentley.'

'Oh, he isn't. Nobody could *like* him. But I don't want to see him hanged for all that.'

'And you think he will be hanged?'

'I don't see why not. His counsel may lodge an appeal — but if so it will be on very flimsy grounds — a technicality of some kind, and I don't see that it will have a chance of success.'

'Did he have a good counsel?'

'Young Graybrook was allotted to him under the Poor Persons' Defence Act. I'd say he was thoroughly conscientious and put up the best show he could.'

'So the man had a fair trial and was condemned by a jury of his fellow-men.'

'That's right. A good average jury. Seven men, five women — all decent reasonable souls. Judge was old Stanisdale. Scrupulously fair — no bias.'

'So — according to the law of the land — James Bentley has nothing to complain of?'

'If he's hanged for something he didn't do, he's got something to complain of!'

'A very just observation.'

'And the case against him was *my* case — I collected the facts and put them together — and it's on that case and those facts that he's been condemned. And I don't like it, M. Poirot, I don't like it.'

Hercule Poirot looked for a long time at the red agitated face of Superintendent Spence.

'*Eh bien*,' he said. 'What do you suggest?'

Spence looked acutely embarrassed.

'I expect you've got a pretty good idea of what's coming. The Bentley case is closed. I'm on another case already — embezzlement. Got to go up to Scotland tonight. I'm not a free man.'

'And I — am?'

Spence nodded in a shame-faced sort of way.

'You've got it. Awful cheek, you'll think. But I can't think of anything else — of any other way. I did all I could at the time, I examined every possibility I could. And I didn't get anywhere. I don't believe I ever would get anywhere. But who knows, it may be different for you. You look at things in — if you'll pardon me for saying so — in a funny sort of way. Maybe that's the way you've got to look at them in this case. Because if James Bentley didn't kill her, then somebody else did. She didn't chop the back of her head in herself. You may be able to find something that I missed. There's no reason why you should do anything about this business. It's infernal cheek my even suggesting such a thing. But there it is. I came to you because it was the only thing I could think of. But if you don't want to put yourself out — and why should you — '

Poirot interrupted him.

'Oh, but indeed there are reasons. I have leisure — too much leisure. And you have intrigued me — yes, you have intrigued me very much. It is a challenge — to the little grey cells of my brain. And then, I have a regard for you. I see you, in your garden in six months' time, planting, perhaps, the rose bushes — and as you plant them it is not with the happiness you should be feeling, because behind everything there is an unpleasantness in your brain, a recollection that you try to push away, and I would not have you feel that, my friend. And finally — ' Poirot sat upright and nodded his head vigorously, 'there is the principle of the thing. If a man has not committed murder, he should not be hanged.' He paused and then added, 'But supposing that after all, he did kill her?'

'In that case I'd be only too thankful to be convinced of it.'

'And two heads are better than one? *Voilà*, everything is settled. I precipitate myself upon the business. There is, that is clear, no time to be lost. Already the scent is cold. Mrs McGinty was killed — when?'

'Last November, 22nd.'

'Then let us at once get down to the brass tacks.'

'I've got my notes on the case which I'll pass over to you.'

'Good. For the moment, we need only the bare outline. If James Bentley did not kill Mrs McGinty, who did?'

Spence shrugged his shoulders and said heavily:

'There's nobody, so far as I can see.'

'But that answer we do not accept. Now, since for every murder there must be a motive, what, in the case of Mrs McGinty, could the motive be? Envy, revenge, jealousy, fear, money? Let us take the last and the simplest? Who profited by her death?'

'Nobody very much. She had two hundred

pounds in the Savings Bank. Her niece gets that.'

'Two hundred pounds is not very much — but in certain circumstances it could be enough. So let us consider the niece. I apologize, my friend, for treading in your footsteps. You too, I know, must have considered all this. But I have to go over with you the ground already traversed.'

Spence nodded his large head.

'We considered the niece, of course. She's thirty-eight, married. Husband is employed in the building and decorating trade — a painter. He's got a good character, steady employment, sharp sort of fellow, no fool. She's a pleasant young woman, a bit talkative, seemed fond of her aunt in a mild sort of way. Neither of them had any urgent need for two hundred pounds, though quite pleased to have it, I dare say.'

'What about the cottage? Do they get that?'

'It was rented. Of course, under the Rent Restriction Act the landlord couldn't get the old woman out. But now she's dead, I don't think the niece could have taken over — anyway she and her husband didn't want to. They've got a small modern council house of their own of which they are extremely proud.' Spence sighed. 'I went into the niece and her husband pretty closely — they seemed the best bet, as you'll understand. But I couldn't get hold of anything.'

'*Bien*. Now let us talk about Mrs McGinty herself. Describe her to me — and not only in physical terms, if you please.'

Spence grinned.

'Don't want a police description? Well, she was sixty-four. Widow. Husband had been employed in the drapery department of Hodges in Kilchester. He died about seven years ago. Pneumonia. Since then, Mrs McGinty has been going out daily to various houses round about. Domestic chores. Broadhinny's a small village which has lately become residential. One or two retired people, one of the partners in an engineering works, a doctor, that sort of thing. There's quite a good bus and train service to Kilchester, and Cullenquay which, as I expect you know, is quite a large summer resort, is only eight miles away, but Broadhinny itself is still quite pretty and rural — about a quarter of a mile off the main Drymouth and Kilchester road.'

Poirot nodded.

'Mrs McGinty's cottage was one of four that form the village proper. There is the post office and village shop, and agricultural labourers live in the others.'

'And she took in a lodger?'

'Yes. Before her husband died, it used to be summer visitors, but after his death she just took one regular. James Bentley had been there for some months.'

'So we come to — James Bentley?'

'Bentley's last job was with a house agent's in Kilchester. Before that, he lived with his mother in Cullenquay. She was an invalid and he looked after her and never went out much. Then she died, and an annuity she had died with her. He sold the little house and found a job. Well educated man, but no special qualifications or aptitudes, and, as I say, an unprepossessing manner. Didn't find it easy to get anything. Anyway, they took him on at Breather & Scuttle's. Rather a second-rate firm. I don't think he was particularly efficient or successful. They cut down staff and he was the one to go. He couldn't get another job, and his money ran out. He usually paid Mrs McGinty every month for his room. She gave him breakfast and supper and charged him three pounds a week — quite reasonable, all things considered. He was two months behind in paying her, and he was nearly at the end of his resources. He hadn't got another job and she was pressing him for what he owed her.'

'And he knew that she had thirty pounds in the house? Why did she have thirty pounds in the house, by the way, since she had a Savings Bank account?'

'Because she didn't trust the Government. Said they'd got two hundred pounds of her money, but they wouldn't get any more. She'd keep that where she could lay her hands on it any minute. She said that to one or two people. It was under a loose board in her bedroom floor — a very obvious place. James Bentley admitted he knew it was there.'

'Very obliging of him. And did niece and husband know that too?'

'Oh yes.'

'Then we have now arrived back at my first question to you. How did Mrs McGinty die?'

'She died on the night of November 22nd. Police surgeon put the time of death as being between 7 and 10 p.m. She'd had her supper — a kipper and bread and margarine, and according to all accounts, she usually had that about half-past six. If she adhered to that on the night in question, then by the evidence of digestion she was killed about eight-thirty or nine o'clock. James Bentley, by his own account, was out walking that evening from seven-fifteen to about nine. He went out and walked most evenings after dark. According to his own story he came in at about nine o'clock (he had his own key) and went straight upstairs to his room. Mrs McGinty had had wash-basins fixed in the bedrooms because of summer visitors. He read for about half an hour and then went to bed. He heard and noticed nothing out of the way. Next morning he came downstairs and looked into the kitchen, but there was no one there and no signs of breakfast being prepared. He says he hesitated a bit and then knocked on Mrs McGinty's door, but got no reply.

'He thought she must have overslept, but didn't like to go on knocking. Then the baker came and James Bentley went up and knocked again, and after that, as I told you, the baker went next door and fetched in a Mrs Elliot, who eventually found the body and went off the deep end. Mrs McGinty was lying on the parlour floor. She'd been hit on the back of the head with something rather in the nature of a meat chopper with a very sharp edge. She'd been killed instantaneously. Drawers were pulled open and things strewn about, and the loose board in the floor in her bedroom had been prised up and the *cache* was empty. All the windows were closed and shuttered on the inside. No signs of anything being tampered with or of being broken into from outside.'

'Therefore,' said Poirot, 'either James Bentley must have killed her, or else she must have admitted her killer herself whilst Bentley was out?'

'Exactly. It wasn't any hold-up or burglar. Now who would she be likely to let in? One of the neighbours, or her niece, or her niece's husband. It boils down to that. We eliminated the neighbours. Niece and her husband were at the pictures that night. It is possible — just possible, that one or other of them left the cinema unobserved, bicycled three miles, killed the old woman, hid the money outside the house, and got back into the cinema unnoticed. We looked into that possibility, but we didn't find any confirmation of it. And why hide the money outside McGinty's house if so? Difficult place to pick it up later. Why not somewhere along the three miles back? No, the only reason for hiding it where it was hidden — '

Poirot finished the sentence for him.

'Would be because you were living in that house, but didn't want to hide it in your room or anywhere inside. In fact: James Bentley.'

'That's right. Everywhere, every time, you came up against Bentley. Finally there was the blood on his cuff.'

'How did he account for that?'

'Said he remembered brushing up against a butcher's shop the previous day. Baloney! It wasn't animal blood.'

'And he stuck to that story?'

'Not likely. At the trial he told a completely different tale. You see, there was a hair on the cuff as well — a blood-stained hair, and the hair was identical with Mrs McGinty's hair. That had got to be explained away. He admitted then that he had gone into the room the night before when he came back from his walk. He'd gone in, he said, after knocking, and found her there, on the floor, dead. He'd bent over and touched her, he said, to make sure. And then he'd lost his head. He'd always been very much affected by the sight of blood, he said. He went to his room in a state of collapse and more or less fainted. In the morning he couldn't bring himself to admit he knew what had happened.'

'A very fishy story,' commented Poirot.

'Yes, indeed. And yet, you know,' said Spence thoughtfully, 'it might well be true. It's not the sort of thing that an ordinary man — or a jury — can believe. But I've come across people like that. I don't mean the collapse story. I mean people who are confronted by a demand for responsible action and who simply can't face up to it. Shy people. He goes in, say, and finds her. He knows that he ought to do something — get the police — go to a neighbour — do the right thing whatever it is. And he funks it. He thinks 'I don't need to know anything about it. I needn't have come in here tonight. I'll go to bed just as if I hadn't come in here at all ... ' Behind it, of course, there's fear — fear that he may be suspected of having a hand in it. He thinks he'll keep himself out of it as long as possible, and so the silly juggins goes and puts himself into it — up to his neck.'

Spence paused.

'It *could* have been that way.'

'It could,' said Poirot thoughtfully.

'Or again, it may have been just the best story his counsel could think up for him. But I don't know. The waitress in the café in Kilchester where he usually had lunch said that he always chose a table where he could look into a wall or a corner and not see people. He was that kind of a chap — just a bit screwy. But not screwy enough to be a killer. He'd no persecution complex or anything of that kind.'

Spence looked hopefully at Poirot — but Poirot did not respond — he was frowning.

The two men sat silent for a while.

3

At last Poirot roused himself with a sigh.

'*Eh bien*,' he said. 'We have exhausted the motive of money. Let us pass to other theories. Had Mrs McGinty an enemy? Was she afraid of anyone?'

'No evidence of it.'

'What did her neighbours have to say?'

'Not very much. They wouldn't to the police, perhaps, but I don't think they were holding anything back. She kept herself to herself, they said. But that's regarded as natural enough. Our villages, you know, M. Poirot, aren't friendly. Evacuees found that during the war. Mrs McGinty passed the time of day with the neighbours but they weren't intimate.'

'How long had she lived there?'

'Matter of eighteen or twenty years, I think.'

'And the forty years before that?'

'There's no mystery about her. Farmer's daughter from North Devon. She and her husband lived near Ilfracombe for a time, and then moved to Kilchester. Had a cottage the other side of it — but found it damp, so they moved to Broadhinny. Husband seems to have been a quiet, decent man, delicate — didn't go to the pub much. All very respectable and above board. No mysteries anywhere, nothing to hide.'

'And yet she was killed?'

'And yet she was killed.'

'The niece didn't know of anyone who had a grudge against her aunt?'

'She says not.'

Poirot rubbed his nose in an exasperated fashion.

'You comprehend, my dear friend, it would be so much easier if Mrs McGinty was *not* Mrs McGinty, so to speak. If she could be what is called a Mystery Woman — a woman with a past.'

'Well, she wasn't,' said Spence stolidly. 'She was just Mrs McGinty, a more or less uneducated woman, who let rooms and went out charring. Thousands of them all over England.'

'But they do not all get murdered.'

'No. I grant you that.'

'So why should Mrs McGinty get murdered? The obvious answer we do not accept. What remains? A shadowy and improbable niece. An even more shadowy and improbable stranger. Facts? Let us stick to facts. What are the facts? An elderly charwoman is murdered. A shy and uncouth young man is arrested and convicted of the murder. Why was James Bentley arrested?'

Spence stared.

'The evidence against him. I've told you — '

'Yes. Evidence. But tell me, my Spence, was it real evidence or was it contrived?'

'Contrived?'

'Yes. Granted the premise that James Bentley is innocent, two possibilities remain. The evidence was manufactured, deliberately, to throw suspicion upon him. Or else he was just the unfortunate victim of circumstances.'

Spence considered.

'Yes. I see what you're driving at.'

'There is nothing to show that the former was the case. But again there is nothing to show that it was not so. The money was taken and hidden outside the house in a place easily found. To have actually hidden it in his room would have been a little too much for the police to swallow. The murder was committed at a time when Bentley was taking a lonely walk, as he often did. Did the bloodstain come on his sleeve as he said it did at his trial, or was that, too, contrived? Did someone brush against him in the darkness and smear tell-tale evidence on his sleeve?'

'I think that's going a bit far, M. Poirot.'

'Perhaps, perhaps. But we have got to go far. I think that in this case we have got to go so far that the imagination cannot as yet see the path clearly . . . For, you see, *mon cher Spence*, if Mrs McGinty is just an ordinary charwoman — it is the *murderer* who must be extraordinary. Yes — that follows clearly. It is in the murderer and not the murdered that the interest of this case lies. That is not the case in most crimes. Usually it is in the personality of the murdered person that the crux of the situation lies. It is the silent dead in whom I am usually interested. Their hates, their loves, their actions. And when you really know the murdered victim, then the victim speaks, and those dead lips utter a name — the name you want to know.'

Spence looked rather uncomfortable.

'Those foreigners!' he seemed to be saying to himself.

'But here,' continued Poirot, 'it is the opposite. Here we guess at a veiled personality — a figure still hidden in darkness. How did Mrs McGinty die? Why did she die? The answer is not to be found in studying the life of Mrs McGinty. The answer is to be found in the personality of the murderer. You agree with me there?'

'I suppose so,' said Superintendent Spence cautiously.

'Someone who wanted — what? To strike down Mrs McGinty? *Or to strike down James Bentley?*'

The Superintendent gave a doubtful 'H'm!'

'Yes — yes, that is one of the first points to be decided. Who is the real victim? Who was intended to be the victim?'

Spence said incredulously: 'You really think someone would bump off a perfectly inoffensive old woman in order to get someone else hanged for murder?'

'One cannot make an omelette, they say, without breaking eggs. Mrs McGinty, then, may be the egg, and James Bentley is the omelette. So let me hear, now, what you know of James Bentley.'

'Nothing much. Father was a doctor — died when Bentley was nine years old. He went to one of the smaller public schools, unfit for the Army, had a weak chest, was in one of the Ministries during the war and lived with a possessive mother.'

'Well,' said Poirot, 'there are certain possibilities there . . . More than there are in the life history of Mrs McGinty.'

'Do you seriously believe what you are suggesting?'

'No, I do not believe anything as yet. But I say that there are two distinct lines of research, and that we have to decide, very soon, which is the right one to follow.'

'How are you going to set about things, M. Poirot? Is there anything I can do?'

'First, I should like an interview with James Bentley.'

'That can be arranged. I'll get on to his solicitors.'

'After that and subject, of course, to the result, if any — I am not hopeful — of that interview, I shall go to Broadhinny. There, aided by your notes, I shall, as quickly as possible, go over that same ground where you have passed before me.'

'In case I've missed anything,' said Spence with a wry smile.

'In case, I would prefer to say, that some circumstance should strike me in a different light to the one in which it struck you. Human reactions vary and so does human experience. The resemblance of a rich financier to a soap boiler whom I had known in Liège once brought about a most satisfactory result. But no need to go into that. What I should like to do is to eliminate one or other of the trails I indicated just now. And to eliminate the Mrs McGinty trail — trail No. 1 — will obviously be quicker and easier than to attack trail No. 2. Where, now, can I stay in Broadhinny? Is there an inn of moderate comfort?'

'There's the Three Ducks — but it doesn't put people up. There's the Lamb in Cullavon three miles away — or there is a kind of a Guest House in Broadhinny itself. It's not really a Guest House, just a rather decrepit country house where the young couple who own it take in paying guests. I don't think,' said Spence dubiously, 'that it's very comfortable.'

Hercule Poirot closed his eyes in agony.

'If I suffer, I suffer,' he said. 'It has to be.'

'I don't know what you'll go there as,' continued Spence doubtfully as he eyed Poirot. 'You might be some kind of an opera singer. Voice broken down. Got to rest. That might do.'

'I shall go,' said Hercule Poirot, speaking with accents of royal blood, 'as myself.'

Spence received this pronouncement with pursed lips.

'D'you think that's advisable?'

'I think it is *essential*! But yes, essential. Consider, *cher ami*, it is *time* we are up against. What do we know? Nothing. So the hope, the best hope, is to go pretending that I know a great deal. I am Hercule Poirot. I am the great, the unique Hercule Poirot. And I, Hercule Poirot, am not satisfied about the verdict in the McGinty case. I, Hercule Poirot, have a very shrewd suspicion of *what*

34

really happened. There is a circumstance that I, alone, estimate at its true value. You see?'

'And then?'

'And then, having made my effect, I observe the reactions. For there should be reactions. Very definitely, there should be reactions.'

Superintendent Spence looked uneasily at the little man.

'Look here, M. Poirot,' he said. 'Don't go sticking out your neck. I don't want anything to happen to you.'

'But if it does, you would be proved right beyond the shadow of doubt, is it not so?'

'I don't want it proved the hard way,' said Superintendent Spence.

4

With great distaste, Hercule Poirot looked round the room in which he stood. It was a room of gracious proportions but there its attraction ended. Poirot made an eloquent grimace as he drew a suspicious finger along the top of a book case. As he had suspected — dust! He sat down gingerly on a sofa and its broken springs sagged depressingly under him. The two faded armchairs were, as he knew, little better. A large fierce-looking dog whom Poirot suspected of having mange growled from his position on a moderately comfortable fourth chair.

The room was large, and had a faded Morris wallpaper. Steel engravings of unpleasant subjects hung crookedly on the walls with one or two good oil paintings. The chair-covers were both faded and dirty, the carpet had holes in it and had never been of a pleasant design. A good deal of miscellaneous bric-à-brac was scattered haphazard here and there. Tables rocked dangerously owing to absence of castors. One window was open, and no power on earth could, apparently, shut it again. The door, temporarily shut, was

not likely to remain so. The latch did not
hold, and with every gust of wind it burst
open and whirling gusts of cold wind eddied
round the room.

'I suffer,' said Hercule Poirot to himself in
acute self-pity. 'Yes, I suffer.'

The door burst open and the wind and
Mrs Summerhayes came in together. She
looked round the room, shouted 'What?' to
someone in the distance and went out again.

Mrs Summerhayes had red hair and an
attractively freckled face and was usually in a
distracted state of putting things down, or
else looking for them.

Hercule Poirot sprang to his feet and shut
the door.

A moment or two later it opened again and
Mrs Summerhayes reappeared. This time she
was carrying a large enamel basin and a knife.

A man's voice from some way away called
out:

'Maureen, that cat's been sick again. What
shall I do?'

Mrs Summerhayes called: 'I'm coming,
darling. Hold everything.'

She dropped the basin and the knife and
went out again.

Poirot got up again and shut the door. He
said:

'Decidedly, I suffer.'

A car drove up, the large dog leaped from the chair and raised its voice in a crescendo of barking. He jumped on a small table by the window and the table collapsed with a crash.

'*Enfin*,' said Hercule Poirot. '*C'est insupportable!*'

The door burst open, the wind surged round the room, the dog rushed out, still barking. Maureen's voice came, upraised loud and clear.

'Johnnie, why the hell did you leave the back door open! Those bloody hens are in the larder.'

'And for this,' said Hercule Poirot with feeling, 'I pay seven guineas a week!'

The door banged to with a crash. Through the window came the loud squawking of irate hens.

Then the door opened again and Maureen Summerhayes came in and fell upon the basin with a cry of joy.

'Couldn't think where I'd left it. Would you mind frightfully, Mr Er — hum — I mean, would it bother you if I sliced the beans in here? The smell in the kitchen is too frightful.'

'Madame, I should be enchanted.'

It was not, perhaps, the exact phrase, but it was near enough. It was the first time in twenty-four hours that Poirot had seen any chance of a conversation of more than six seconds' duration.

Mrs Summerhayes flung herself down in a chair and began slicing beans with frenzied energy and considerable awkwardness.

'I do hope,' she said, 'that you're not too frightfully uncomfortable? If there's anything you want altered, do say so.'

Poirot had already come to the opinion that the only thing in Long Meadows he could even tolerate was his hostess.

'You are too kind, madame,' he replied politely. 'I only wish it were within my powers to provide you with suitable domestics.'

'Domestics!' Mrs Summerhayes gave a squeal. 'What a hope! Can't even get hold of a *daily*. Our really good one was murdered. Just my luck.'

'That would be Mrs McGinty,' said Poirot quickly.

'Mrs McGinty it was. God, how I miss that woman! Of course it was all a big thrill at the time. First murder we've ever had right in the family, so to speak, but as I told Johnnie, it was a downright bit of bad luck for us. Without McGinty I just can't cope.'

'You were attached to her?'

'My dear man, she was *reliable*. She *came*. Monday afternoons and Thursday mornings — just like a clock. Now I have that Burp woman from up by the station. Five children and a husband. Naturally she's never here. Either the husband's taken queer, or the old mother, or the children have some foul disease or other. With old McGinty, at least it was only she herself who came over queer, and I must say she hardly ever did.'

'And you found her always reliable and honest? You had trust in her?'

'Oh, she'd never pinch anything — not even food. Of course she snooped a bit. Had a look at one's letters and all that. But one expects that sort of thing. I mean they must live such awfully drab lives, mustn't they?'

'Had Mrs McGinty had a drab life?'

'Ghastly, I expect,' said Mrs Summerhayes vaguely. 'Always on your knees scrubbing. And then piles of other people's washing-up waiting for you on the sink when you arrive in the morning. If I had to face that every day, I'd be positively relieved to be murdered. I really would.'

The face of Major Summerhayes appeared at the window. Mrs Summerhayes sprang up, upsetting the beans, and rushed across to the window, which she opened to the fullest extent.

'That damned dog's eaten the hens' food again, Maureen.'

'Oh damn, now *he'll* be sick!'

'Look here,' John Summerhayes displayed a

colander full of greenery, 'is this enough spinach?'

'Of course not.'

'Seems a colossal amount to me.'

'It'll be about a teaspoonful when it's cooked. Don't you know by now what spinach is like?'

'Oh Lord!'

'Has the fish come?'

'Not a sign of it.'

'Hell, we'll have to open a tin of something. You might do that, Johnnie. One of the ones in the corner cupboard. That one we thought was a bit bulged. I expect it's quite all right really.'

'What about the spinach?'

'I'll get that.'

She leaped through the window, and husband and wife moved away together.

'*Nom d'un nom d'un nom!*' said Hercule Poirot. He crossed the room and closed the window as nearly as he could. The voice of Major Summerhayes came to him borne on the wind.

'What about this new fellow, Maureen? Looks a bit peculiar to me. What's his name again?'

'I couldn't remember it just now when I was talking to him. Had to say Mr Er-um. Poirot — that's what it is. He's French.'

'You know, Maureen, I seem to have seen that name somewhere.'

'Home Perm, perhaps. He looks like a hairdresser.' Poirot winced.

'N-no. Perhaps it's pickles. I don't know. I'm sure it's familiar. Better get the first seven guineas out of him, quick.'

The voices died away.

Hercule Poirot picked up the beans from the floor where they had scattered far and wide. Just as he finished doing so, Mrs Summerhayes came in again through the door.

He presented them to her politely:

'*Voici, madame.*'

'Oh, thanks awfully. I say, these beans look a bit black. We store them, you know, in crocks, salted down. But these seem to have gone wrong. I'm afraid they won't be very nice.'

'I, too, fear that . . . You permit that I shut the door? There is a decided draught.'

'Oh yes, do. I'm afraid I always leave doors open.'

'So I have noticed.'

'Anyway, that door never stays shut. This house is practically falling to pieces. Johnnie's father and mother lived here and they were badly off, poor dears, and they never did a thing to it. And then when we came home from India to live here, we couldn't afford to do anything either. It's fun for the children in the holidays, though, lots of room to run wild in, and the garden and everything. Having paying guests here just enables us to keep going, though I must say we've had a few rude shocks.'

'Am I your only guest at present?'

'We've got an old lady upstairs. Took to her bed the day she came and has been there ever since. Nothing the matter with her that I can see. But there she is, and I carry up four trays a day. Nothing wrong with her appetite. Anyway, she's going tomorrow to some niece or other.'

Mrs Summerhayes paused for a moment before resuming in a slightly artificial voice.

'The fishman will be here in a minute. I wonder if you'd mind — er — forking out the first week's rent. You are staying a week, aren't you?'

'Perhaps longer.'

'Sorry to bother you. But I've not got any cash in the house and you know what these people are like — always dunning you.'

'Pray do not apologize, madame.' Poirot took out seven pound notes and added seven shillings. Mrs Summerhayes gathered the money up with avidity.

'Thanks a lot.'

'I should, perhaps, madame, tell you a little more about myself. *I am Hercule Poirot.*'

The revelation left Mrs Summerhayes unmoved.

'What a lovely name,' she said kindly. 'Greek, isn't it?'

'I am, as you may know,' said Poirot, 'a detective.' He tapped his chest. 'Perhaps the most famous detective there is.'

Mrs Summerhayes screamed with amusement.

'I see you're a great practical joker, M. Poirot. What are you detecting? Cigarette ash and footprints?'

'I am investigating the murder of Mrs McGinty,' said Poirot. 'And I do not joke.'

'Ouch,' said Mrs Summerhayes, 'I've cut my hand.'

She raised a finger and inspected it.

Then she stared at Poirot.

'Look here,' she said. 'Do you mean it? What I mean is, it's all over, all that. They arrested that poor half-wit who lodged there and he's been tried and convicted and everything. He's probably been hanged by now.'

'No, madame,' said Poirot. 'He has not been hanged — yet. And it is not 'over' — the case of Mrs McGinty. I will remind you of the line from one of your poets. 'A question is never settled until it is settled — right.' '

'Oo,' said Mrs Summerhayes, her attention diverted from Poirot to the basin in her lap. 'I'm bleeding over the beans. Not too good as we've got to have them for lunch. Still it won't matter really because they'll go into boiling water. Things are always all right if you boil them, aren't they? Even tins.'

'I think,' said Hercule Poirot quietly, 'that I shall not be in for lunch.'

5

'I don't know, I'm sure,' said Mrs Burch.

She had said that three times already. Her natural distrust of foreign-looking gentlemen with black moustaches, wearing large fur-lined coats, was not to be easily overcome.

'Very unpleasant, it's been,' she went on. 'Having poor auntie murdered and the police and all that. Tramping round everywhere, and ferreting about, and asking questions. With the neighbours all agog. I didn't feel at first we'd ever live it down. And my husband's mother's been downright nasty about it. Nothing of that kind ever happened in *her* family, she kept saying. And 'poor Joe' and all that. What about poor me? She was *my* aunt, wasn't she? But really I did think it was all over now.'

'And supposing that James Bentley is innocent, after all?'

'Nonsense,' snapped Mrs Burch. 'Of course he isn't innocent. He did it all right. I never did like the looks of him. Wandering about muttering to himself. Said to auntie, I did: 'You oughtn't to have a man like that in the house. Might go off his head,' I said. But she said he was quiet and obliging and didn't give trouble. No drinking, she said, and he didn't even smoke. Well, she knows better now, poor soul.'

Poirot looked thoughtfully at her. She was a big, plump woman with a healthy colour and a good-humoured mouth. The small house was neat and clean and smelt of furniture polish and Brasso. A faint appetizing smell came from the direction of the kitchen.

A good wife who kept her house clean and took the trouble to cook for her man. He approved. She was prejudiced and obstinate but, after all, why not? Most decidedly, she was not the kind of woman one could imagine using a meat chopper on her aunt, or conniving at her husband's doing so. Spence had not thought her that kind of woman, and rather reluctantly, Hercule Poirot agreed with him. Spence had gone into the financial background of the Burches and had found no motive there for murder, and Spence was a very thorough man.

He sighed, and persevered with his task, which was the breaking down of Mrs Burch's suspicion of foreigners. He led the conversation away from murder and focused on the victim of it. He asked questions about 'poor auntie', her health, her habits, her preferences in food and drink, her politics, her late husband, her attitude to life, to sex, to sin, to religion, to children, to animals.

Whether any of this irrelevant matter would be of use, he had no idea. He was looking through a haystack to find a needle. But, incidentally, he was learning something about Bessie Burch.

Bessie did not really know very much about her aunt. It had been a family tie, honoured as such, but without intimacy. Now and again, once a month or so, she and Joe had gone over on a Sunday to have midday dinner with auntie, and more rarely, auntie had come over to see them. They had exchanged presents at Christmas. They'd known that auntie had a little something put by, and that they'd get it when she died.

'But that's not to say we were needing it,' Mrs Burch explained with rising colour. 'We've got something put by ourselves. And we buried her beautiful. A real nice funeral it was. Flowers and everything.'

Auntie had been fond of knitting. She didn't like dogs, they messed up a place, but she used to have a cat — a ginger. It strayed away and she hadn't had one since, but the woman at the post office had been going to give her a kitten. Kept her house very neat and didn't like litter. Kept brass a treat and washed down the kitchen floor every day. She made quite a nice thing of going out to work. One shilling and tenpence an hour — two shillings from Holmeleigh, that was Mr Carpenter's of the Works' house. Rolling in money, the Carpenters were. Tried to get auntie to come more days in the week, but auntie wouldn't disappoint her other ladies because she'd gone to them before she went to Mr Carpenter's, and it wouldn't have been right.

Poirot mentioned Mrs Summerhayes at Long Meadows.

Oh yes, auntie went to her — two days a week. They'd come back from India where they'd had a lot of native servants and Mrs Summerhayes didn't know a thing about a house. They tried to market-garden, but they didn't know anything about that, either. When the children came home for the holidays, the house was just pandemonium. But Mrs Summerhayes was a nice lady and auntie liked her.

So the portrait grew. Mrs McGinty knitted, and scrubbed floors and polished brass, she liked cats and didn't like dogs. She liked children, but not very much. She kept herself to herself.

She attended church on Sunday, but didn't take part in any church activities. Sometimes, but rarely, she went to the pictures. She didn't hold with goings on — and had given up working for an artist and his wife when she discovered they weren't properly married. She didn't read books, but she enjoyed the Sunday paper and she liked old magazines when her ladies gave them to her. Although she didn't go much to the pictures, she was interested in hearing about film stars and their doings. She wasn't interested in politics, but voted Conservative like her husband had always done. Never spent much on clothes, but got quite a lot given her from her ladies, and was of a saving disposition.

Mrs McGinty was, in fact, very much the Mrs McGinty that Poirot had imagined she would be. And Bessie Burch, her niece, was the Bessie Burch of Superintendent Spence's notes.

Before Poirot took his leave, Joe Burch came home for the lunch hour. A small, shrewd man, less easy to be sure about than his wife. There was a faint nervousness in his manner. He showed less signs of suspicion and hostility than his wife. Indeed he seemed anxious to appear cooperative. And that, Poirot reflected, was very faintly out of character. For why should Joe Burch be anxious to placate an importunate foreign stranger? The reason could only be that the stranger had brought with him a letter from

Superintendent Spence of the County Police.

So Joe Burch was anxious to stand in well with the police? Was it that he couldn't afford, as his wife could, to be critical of the police?

A man, perhaps, with an uneasy conscience. Why was that conscience uneasy? There could be so many reasons — none of them connected with Mrs McGinty's death. Or was it that, somehow or other, the cinema alibi had been cleverly faked, and that it was Joe Burch who had knocked on the door of the cottage, had been admitted by auntie and who had struck down the unsuspecting old woman? He would pull out the drawers and ransack the rooms to give the appearance of robbery, he might hide the money outside, cunningly, to incriminate James Bentley, the money that was in the Savings Bank was what he was after. Two hundred pounds coming to his wife which, for some reason unknown, he badly needed. The weapon, Poirot remembered, had never been found. Why had that not also been found on the scene of the crime? Any moron knew enough to wear gloves or rub off fingerprints. Why then had the weapon, which must have been a heavy one with a sharp edge, been removed? Was it because it could easily be identified as belonging to the Burch ménage? Was that same weapon, washed and polished, here in the house now? Something in the nature of a meat chopper, the police surgeon had said — but not, it seemed, actually a meat chopper. Something, perhaps a little unusual ... a little out of the ordinary, easily identified. The police had hunted for it, but not found it. They had searched woods, dragged ponds. There was nothing missing from Mrs McGinty's kitchen, and nobody could say that James Bentley had had anything of that kind in his possession. They had never traced any purchase of a meat chopper or any such implement to him. A small, but negative point in his favour. Ignored in the weight of other evidence. But still a point ...

Poirot cast a swift glance round the rather overcrowded little sitting-room in which he was sitting.

Was the weapon here, somewhere, in this house? Was that why Joe Burch was uneasy and conciliatory?

Poirot did not know. He did not really think so. But he was not absolutely sure ...

6

I

In the offices of Messrs Breather & Scuttle, Poirot was shown, after some demur, into the room of Mr Scuttle himself.

Mr Scuttle was a brisk, bustling man, with a hearty manner.

'Good morning. Good morning.' He rubbed his hands. 'Now, what can we do for you?'

His professional eye shot over Poirot, trying to place him, making, as it were, a series of marginal notes.

Foreign. Good quality clothes. Probably rich. Restaurant proprietor? Hotel manager? Films?

'I hope not to trespass on your time unduly. I wanted to talk to you about your former employee, James Bentley.'

Mr Scuttle's expressive eyebrows shot up an inch and dropped.

'James Bentley. James Bentley?' He shot out a question. 'Press?'

'No.'

'And you wouldn't be police?'

'No. At least — not of this country.'

'Not of this country.' Mr Scuttle filed this away rapidly as though for future reference. 'What's it all about?'

Poirot, never hindered by a pedantic regard for truth, launched out into speech.

'I am opening a further inquiry into James Bentley's case — at the request of certain relatives of his.'

'Didn't know he had any. Anyway, he's been found guilty, you know, and condemned to death.'

'But not yet executed.'

'While there's life, there's hope, eh?' Mr Scuttle shook his head. 'Should doubt it, though. Evidence was strong. Who are these relations of his?'

'I can only tell you this, they are both rich and powerful. Immensely rich.'

'You surprise me.' Mr Scuttle was unable to help thawing slightly. The words 'immensely rich' had an attractive and hypnotic quality. 'Yes, you really do surprise me.'

'Bentley's mother, the late Mrs Bentley,' explained Poirot, 'cut herself and her son off completely from her family.'

'One of these family feuds, eh? Well, well. And young Bentley without a farthing to bless himself with. Pity these relations didn't come to the rescue before.'

'They have only just become aware of the facts,' explained Poirot. 'They have engaged me to come with all speed to this country and do everything possible.'

Mr Scuttle leaned back, relaxing his business manner.

'Don't know what you can do. I suppose there's insanity? A bit late in the day — but if you got hold of the big medicos. Of course I'm not up in these things myself.'

Poirot leaned forward.

'Monsieur, James Bentley worked here. You can tell me about him.'

'Precious little to tell — precious little. He was one of our junior clerks. Nothing against him. Seemed a perfectly decent young fellow, quite conscientious and all that. But no idea of salesmanship. He just couldn't put a project over. That's no good in this job. If a client comes to us with a house he wants to sell, we're there to sell it for him. And if a client wants a house, we find him one. If it's a house in a lonely place with no amenities, we stress its antiquity, call it a period piece — and don't mention the plumbing! And if the house looks straight into the gasworks, we talk about amenities and facilities and don't mention the view. Hustle your client into it — that's what you're here to do. All sorts of little tricks there are. 'We advise you, madam, to make an immediate offer. There's a Member of Parliament who's very keen on it — very keen indeed. Going out to see it again this afternoon.' They fall for that every time — a Member of Parliament is always a good touch. Can't think why! No member ever lives away from his constituency. It's just the good solid sound of it.' He laughed suddenly, displayed gleaming dentures. 'Psychology — that's what it is — just psychology.'

Poirot leapt at the word.

'Psychology. How right you are. I see that you are a judge of men.'

'Not too bad. Not too bad,' said Mr Scuttle modestly.

'So I ask you again what was your impression of James Bentley? Between ourselves — strictly between ourselves — you think he killed the old woman?'

Scuttle stared.

'Of course.'

'And you think, too, that it was a likely thing for him to do — psychologically speaking?'

'Well — if you put it like that — no, not really. Shouldn't have thought he had the guts. Tell you what, if you ask me, he was barmy. Put it that way, and it works. Always a bit soft in the head, and what with being out of a job and worrying and all that, he just went right over the edge.'

'You had no special reason for discharging him?'

Scuttle shook his head.

'Bad time of year. Staff hadn't enough to do. We sacked the one who was least competent. That was Bentley. Always would be, I expect. Gave him a good reference and all that. He didn't get another job, though. No pep. Made a bad impression on people.'

It always came back to that, Poirot thought, as he left the office. James Bentley made a bad impression on people. He took comfort in considering various murderers he had known whom most people had found full of charm.

II

'Excuse me, do you mind if I sit down here and talk to you for a moment?'

Poirot, ensconced at a small table in the Blue Cat, looked up from the menu he was studying with a start. It was rather dark in the Blue Cat, which specialized in an old-world effect of oak and leaded panes, but the young woman who had just sat down opposite to him stood out brightly from her dark background.

She had determinedly golden hair, and was wearing an electric blue jumper suit. Moreover, Hercule Poirot was conscious of having noticed her somewhere only a short time previously.

She went on:

'I couldn't help, you see, hearing something of what you were saying to Mr Scuttle.'

Poirot nodded. He had realized that the partitions in the offices of Breather & Scuttle were made for convenience rather than privacy. That had not worried him, since it was chiefly publicity that he desired.

'You were typing,' he said, 'to the right of the back window.'

She nodded. Her teeth shone white in an acquiescing smile. A very healthy young woman, with a full buxom figure that Poirot approved. About thirty-three or four, he judged, and by nature dark-haired, but not one to be dictated to by nature.

'About Mr Bentley,' she said.

'What about Mr Bentley?'

'Is he going to appeal? Does it mean that there's new evidence? Oh, I'm so glad. I couldn't — I just couldn't believe he did it.'

Poirot's eyebrows rose.

'So you never thought he did it,' he said slowly.

'Well, not at first. I thought it must be a mistake. But then the evidence — ' She stopped.

'Yes, the evidence,' said Poirot.

'There just didn't seem anyone else who could have done it. I thought perhaps he'd gone a little mad.'

'Did he ever seem to you a little — what shall I say — queer?'

'Oh no. Not queer in that way. He was just shy and awkward as anyone might be. The truth was, he didn't make the best of himself. He hadn't confidence in himself.'

Poirot looked at her. She certainly had confidence in herself. Possibly she had enough confidence for two.

'You liked him?' he asked.

She flushed.

'Yes, I did. Amy — that's the other girl in the office — used to laugh at him and call him a drip, but I liked him very much. He was gentle and polite — and he knew a lot really. Things out of books, I mean.'

'Ah yes, things out of books.'

'He missed his mother. She'd been ill for years, you know. At least, not really ill, but not strong, and he'd done everything for her.'

Poirot nodded. He knew those mothers.

'And of course she'd looked after him, too. I mean taken care of his health and his chest in winter and what he ate and all that.'

Again he nodded. He asked:

'You and he were friends?'

'I don't know — not exactly. We used to talk sometimes. But after he left here, he — I — I didn't see much of him. I wrote to him once in a friendly way, but he didn't answer.'

Poirot said gently:

'But you like him?'

She said rather defiantly:

'Yes, I do . . . '

'That is excellent,' said Poirot.

His mind switched back to the day of his interview with the condemned prisoner . . . He saw James Bentley clearly. The mouse-coloured hair, the thin awkward body, the hands with their big knuckles and wrists, the Adam's apple in the lean neck. He saw the furtive, embarrassed — almost sly glance. Not straightforward, not a man whose word could be trusted — a secretive, sly deceitful fellow with an ungracious, muttering way of talking . . . That was the impression James Bentley would give to most superficial observers. It was the impression he had given in the dock. The sort of fellow who would tell lies, and steal money, and hit an old woman over the head . . .

But on Superintendent Spence, who knew men, he had not made that impression. Nor on Hercule Poirot . . . And now here was this girl.

'What is your name, mademoiselle?' he asked.

'Maude Williams. Is there anything I could do — to help?'

'I think there is. There are people who believe, Miss Williams, that James Bentley is innocent. They are working to prove that fact. I am the person charged with that investigation, and I may tell you that I have already made considerable progress — yes, considerable progress.'

He uttered that lie without a blush. To his mind it was a very necessary lie. Someone, somewhere, had got to be made uneasy. Maude Williams would talk, and talk was like a stone in a pond, it made a ripple that went on spreading outwards.

He said: 'You tell me that you and James Bentley talked together. He told you about his mother and his home life. Did he ever mention anyone with whom he, or perhaps his mother, was on bad terms?'

Maude Williams reflected.

'No — not what you'd call bad terms. His mother didn't like young women much, I gather.'

'Mothers of devoted sons never like young women. No, I mean more than that. Some family feud, some enmity. Someone with a grudge?'

She shook her head.

'He never mentioned anything of that kind.'

'Did he ever speak of his landlady, Mrs McGinty?'

She shivered slightly.

'Not by name. He said once that she gave him kippers much too often — and once he said his landlady was upset because she had lost her cat.'

'Did he ever — you must be honest, please — mention that he knew where she kept her money?'

Some of the colour went out of the girl's face, but she threw up her chin defiantly.

'Actually, he did. We were talking about people being distrustful of banks — and he said his old landlady kept her spare money under a floorboard. He said: 'I could help myself any day to it when she's out.' Not quite as a joke, he didn't joke, more as though he were really worried by her carelessness.'

'Ah,' said Poirot. 'That is good. From my point of view, I mean. When James Bentley thinks of stealing, it presents itself to him as an action that is done behind someone's back. He might have said, you see, 'Some day someone will knock her on the head for it.' '

'But either way, he wouldn't be meaning it.'

'Oh no. But talk, however light, however idle, gives away, inevitably, the sort of person you are. The wise criminal would never open his mouth, but criminals are seldom wise and usually vain and they talk a good deal — and so most criminals are caught.'

Maude Williams said abruptly:

'But *someone* must have killed the old woman.'

'Naturally.'

'Who did? Do you know? Have you any idea?'

'Yes,' said Hercule Poirot mendaciously. 'I think I have a very good idea. But we are only at the beginning of the road.'

The girl glanced at her watch.

'I must get back. We're only supposed to take half an hour. One-horse place, Kilchester — I've always had jobs in London before. You'll let me know if there's anything I can do — really *do*, I mean?'

Poirot took out one of his cards. On it he wrote Long Meadows and the telephone number.

'That is where I am staying.'

His name, he noted with chagrin, made no

particular impression on her. The younger generation, he could not but feel, were singularly lacking in knowledge of notable celebrities.

III

Hercule Poirot caught a bus back to Broadhinny feeling slightly more cheerful. At any rate there was one person who shared his belief in James Bentley's innocence. Bentley was not so friendless as he had made himself out to be.

His mind went back again to Bentley in prison. What a dispiriting interview it had been. There had been no hope aroused, hardly a stirring of interest.

'Thank you,' Bentley had said dully, 'but I don't suppose there is anything anyone can do.'

No, he was sure he had not got any enemies.

'When people barely notice you're alive, you're not likely to have any enemies.'

'Your mother? Did she have an enemy?'

'Certainly not. Everyone liked and respected her.'

There was a faint indignation in his tone.

'What about your friends?'

64

And James Bentley had said, or rather muttered, 'I haven't any friends . . . '

But that had not been quite true. For Maude Williams was a friend.

'What a wonderful dispensation it is of Nature's,' thought Hercule Poirot, 'that every man, however superficially unattractive, should be some woman's choice.'

For all Miss Williams's sexy appearance, he had a shrewd suspicion that she was really the maternal type.

She had the qualities that James Bentley lacked, the energy, the drive, the refusal to be beaten, the determination to succeed.

He sighed.

What monstrous lies he had told that day! Never mind — they were necessary.

'For somewhere,' said Poirot to himself, indulging in an absolute riot of mixed metaphors, 'there is in the hay a needle, and among the sleeping dogs there is one on whom I shall put my foot, and by shooting the arrows into the air, one will come down and hit a glass-house!'

7

The cottage where Mrs McGinty had lived was only a few steps from the bus stop. Two children were playing on the doorstep. One was eating a rather wormy-looking apple and the other was shouting and beating on the door with a tin tray. They appeared quite happy. Poirot added to the noise by beating hard on the door himself.

A woman looked round the corner of the house. She had on a coloured overall and her hair was untidy.

'Stop it, Ernie,' she said.

'Sha'n't,' said Ernie and continued.

Poirot deserted the doorstep and made for the corner of the house.

'Can't do anything with children, can you?' the woman said.

Poirot thought you could, but forbore to say so.

He was beckoned round to the back door.

'I keep the front bolted up, sir. Come in, won't you?'

Poirot passed through a very dirty scullery into an almost more dirty kitchen.

'She wasn't killed here,' said the woman. 'In the parlour.'

Poirot blinked slightly.

'That's what you're down about, isn't it? You're the foreign gentleman from up at Summerhayes?'

'So you know all about me?' said Poirot. He beamed. 'Yes, indeed, Mrs — '

'Kiddle. My husband's a plasterer. Moved in four months ago, we did. Been living with Bert's mother before . . . Some folks said: 'You'd never go into a house where there's been a murder, surely?' — but what I said was, a house is a house, and better than a back sitting-room and sleeping on two chairs. Awful, this 'ousing shortage, isn't it? And anyway *we've* never been troubled 'ere. Always say they *walk* if they've been murdered, but she doesn't! Like to see where it happened?'

Feeling like a tourist being taken on a conducted tour, Poirot assented.

Mrs Kiddle led him into a small room over-burdened with a heavy Jacobean suite. Unlike the rest of the house, it showed no signs of ever having been occupied.

'Down on the floor she was and the back of her head split open. Didn't half give Mrs

Elliot a turn. She's the one what found her — she and Larkin who comes from the Co-op with the bread. But the money was took from upstairs. Come along up and I'll show you where.'

Mrs Kiddle led the way up the staircase and into a bedroom which contained a large chest of drawers, a big brass bed, some chairs, and a fine assembly of baby clothes, wet and dry.

'Right here it was,' said Mrs Kiddle proudly.

Poirot looked round him. Hard to visualize that this rampant stronghold of haphazard fecundity was once the well-scrubbed domain of an elderly woman who was house-proud. Here Mrs McGinty had lived and slept.

'I suppose this isn't her furniture?'

'Oh no. Her niece over in Cullavon took away all that.'

There was nothing left here of Mrs McGinty. The Kiddles had come and conquered. Life was stronger than death.

From downstairs the loud fierce wail of a baby arose.

'That's the baby woken up,' said Mrs Kiddle unnecessarily.

She plunged down the stairs and Poirot followed her.

There was nothing here for him.

He went next door.

II

'Yes, sir, it was me found her.'

Mrs Elliot was dramatic. A neat house, this, neat and prim. The only drama in it was Mrs Elliot's, a tall gaunt dark-haired woman, recounting her one moment of glorious living.

'Larkin, the baker, he came and knocked at the door. 'It's Mrs McGinty,' he said, 'we can't make her hear. Seems she might have been taken bad.' And indeed I thought she might. She wasn't a young woman, not by any means. And palpitations she'd had, to my certain knowledge. I thought she might have had a stroke. So I hurried over, seeing as there were only the two men, and naturally they wouldn't like to go into the bedroom.'

Poirot accepted this piece of propriety with an assenting murmur.

'Hurried up the stairs, I did. *He* was on the landing, pale as death he was. Not that I ever thought at the time — well, of course, then I didn't know what had happened. I knocked on the door loud and there wasn't any answer, so I turned the handle and I went in.

The whole place messed about — and the board in the floor up. 'It's robbery,' I said. 'But where's the poor soul herself?' And then we thought to look in the sitting-room. *And there she was* . . . Down on the floor with her poor head stove in. Murder! I saw at once what it was — murder! Couldn't be anything else! Robbery and murder! Here in Broadhinny. I screamed and I screamed! Quite a job they had with me. Come over all faint, I did. They had to go and get me brandy from the Three Ducks. And even then I was all of a shiver for hours and hours. 'Don't you take on so, mother,' that's what the sergeant said to me when he came. 'Don't you take on so. You go home and make yourself a nice cup of tea.' And so I did. And when Elliot came home, 'Why, whatever's happened?' he says, staring at me. Still all of a tremble I was. Always was sensitive from a child.'

Poirot dexterously interrupted this thrilling personal narrative.

'Yes, yes, one can see that. And when was the last time you had seen poor Mrs McGinty?'

'Must have been the day before, when she'd stepped out into the back garden to pick a bit of mint. I was just feeding the chickens.'

'Did she say anything to you?'

'Just good afternoon and were they laying any better.'

'And that's the last time you saw her? You didn't see her on the day she died?'

'No. I saw *Him* though.' Mrs Elliot lowered her voice. 'About eleven o'clock in the morning. Just walking along the road. Shuffling his feet the way he always did.'

Poirot waited, but it seemed that there was nothing to add.

He asked:

'Were you surprised when the police arrested him?'

'Well, I was and I wasn't. Mind you, I'd always thought he was a bit daft. And no doubt about it, these daft ones do turn nasty, sometimes. My uncle had a feeble-minded boy, and he could go very nasty sometimes — as he grew up, that was. Didn't know his strength. Yes, that Bentley was daft all right, and I shouldn't be surprised if they don't hang him when it comes to it, but sends him to the asylum instead. Why, look at the place he hid the money. No one would hide money in a place like that unless he wanted it to be found. Just silly and simple like, that's what he was.'

'Unless he wanted it found,' murmured Poirot. 'You did not, by any chance, miss a chopper — or an axe?'

'No, sir, I did *not*. The police asked me that. Asked all of us in the cottages here. It's a mystery still what he killed her with.'

III

Hercule Poirot walked towards the post office.

The murderer had wanted the money found, but he had not wanted the weapon to be found. For the money would point to James Bentley and the weapon would point to — whom?

He shook his head. He had visited the other two cottages. They had been less exuberant than Mrs Kiddle and less dramatic than Mrs Elliot. They had said in effect that Mrs McGinty was a very respectable woman who kept herself to herself, that she had a niece over at Cullavon, that nobody but the said niece ever came to see her, that nobody, so far as they knew, disliked her or bore a grudge against her, that was it true that there was a petition being got up for James Bentley and would they be asked to sign it?

'I get nowhere — nowhere,' said Poirot to himself. 'There is nothing — no little gleam, I can well understand the despair of Superintendent Spence. But it should be different for *me*. Superintendent Spence, he is a good and painstaking police officer, but me, I am Hercule Poirot. For *me*, there should be illumination!'

One of his patent leather shoes slopped into a puddle and he winced.

He was the great, the unique Hercule Poirot, but he was also a very old man and his shoes were tight.

He entered the post office.

The right-hand side was given to the business of His Majesty's mails. The left-hand side displayed a rich assortment of varied merchandise, comprising sweets, groceries, toys, hardware, stationery, birthday cards, knitting wool and children's underclothes.

Poirot proceeded to a leisurely purchase of stamps.

The woman who bustled forward to attend to him was middle-aged with sharp, bright eyes.

'Here,' said Poirot to himself, 'is undoubtedly the brains of the village of Broadhinny.'

Her name, not inappropriately, was Mrs Sweetiman.

'And twelve pennies,' said Mrs Sweetiman, deftly extracting them from a large book. 'That's four and tenpence altogether. Will there be anything more, sir?'

She fixed a bright eager glance at him.

Through the door at the back a girl's head showed listening avidly. She had untidy hair and a cold in the head.

'I am by way of being a stranger in these parts,' said Poirot solemnly.

'That's right, sir,' agreed Mrs Sweetiman. 'Come down from London, haven't you?'

'I expect you know my business here as well as I do,' said Poirot with a slight smile.

'Oh no, sir, I've really no idea,' said Mrs Sweetiman in a wholly perfunctory manner.

'Mrs McGinty,' said Poirot.

Mrs Sweetiman shook her head.

'That was a sad business — a shocking business.'

'I expect you knew her well?'

'Oh I did. As well as anyone in Broadhinny, I should say. She'd always pass the time of day with me when she came in here for any little thing. Yes, it was a terrible tragedy. And not settled yet, or so I've heard people say.'

'There is a doubt — in some quarters — as to James Bentley's guilt.'

'Well,' said Mrs Sweetiman, 'it wouldn't be the first time the police got hold of the wrong man — though I wouldn't say they had in this case. Not that I should have thought it of him really. A shy, awkward sort of fellow, but not dangerous or so you'd think. But there, you never know, do you?'

Poirot hazarded a request for notepaper.

'Of course, sir. Just come across the other side, will you?'

Mrs Sweetiman bustled round to take her place behind the left-hand counter.

'What's difficult to imagine is, who it could have been if it wasn't Mr Bentley,' she remarked as she stretched up to a top shelf for notepaper and envelopes. 'We do get some nasty tramps along here sometimes, and it's possible one of these might have found a window unfastened and got in that way. But he wouldn't go leaving the money behind him, would he? Not after doing murder to get it — and pound notes anyway, nothing with numbers or marked. Here you are, sir, that's a nice blue Bond, and envelopes to match.'

Poirot made his purchase.

'Mrs McGinty never spoke of being nervous of anyone, or afraid, did she?' he asked.

'Not to me, she didn't. She wasn't a nervous woman. She'd stay late sometimes at Mr Carpenter's — that's Holmeleigh at the top of the hill. They often have people to dinner and stopping with them, and Mrs McGinty would go there in the evening sometimes to help wash up, and she'd come down the hill in the dark, and that's more

75

than I'd like to do. Very dark it is — coming down that hill.'

'Do you know her niece at all — Mrs Burch?'

'I know her just to speak to. She and her husband come over sometimes.'

'They inherited a little money when Mrs McGinty died.'

The piercing dark eyes looked at him severely.

'Well, that's natural enough, isn't it, sir? You can't take it with you, and it's only right your own flesh and blood should get it.'

'Oh yes, oh yes, I am entirely in agreement. Was Mrs McGinty fond of her niece?'

'Very fond of her, I think, sir. In a quiet way.'

'And her niece's husband?'

An evasive look appeared in Mrs Sweetiman's face.

'As far as I know.'

'When did you see Mrs McGinty last?'

Mrs Sweetiman considered, casting her mind back.

'Now let me see, when was it, Edna?' Edna, in the doorway, sniffed unhelpfully. 'Was it the day she died? No, it was the day before — or the day before that again? Yes, it was a Monday. That's right. She was killed on the Wednesday. Yes, it was Monday. She came in

76

to buy a bottle of ink.'

'She wanted a bottle of ink?'

'Expect she wanted to write a letter,' said Mrs Sweetiman brightly.

'That seems probable. And she was quite her usual self, then? She did not seem different in any way?'

'N-no, I don't think so.'

The sniffing Edna shuffled through the door into the shop and suddenly joined in the conversation.

'She was different,' she asserted. 'Pleased about something — well — not quite pleased — excited.'

'Perhaps you're right,' said Mrs Sweetiman. 'Not that I noticed it at the time. But now that you say so — sort of spry, she was.'

'Do you remember anything she said on that day?'

'I wouldn't ordinarily. But what with her being murdered and the police and every-thing, it makes things stand out. She didn't say anything about James Bentley, that I'm quite sure. Talked about the Carpenters a bit and Mrs Upward — places where she worked, you know.'

'Oh yes, I was going to ask you whom exactly she worked for here.'

Mrs Sweetiman replied promptly:

'Mondays and Thursdays she went to Mrs

Summerhayes at Long Meadow. That's where you are staying, isn't it?'

'Yes,' Poirot sighed, 'I suppose there is not anywhere else to stay?'

'Not right in Broadhinny, there isn't. I suppose you aren't very comfortable at Long Meadows? Mrs Summerhayes is a nice lady but she doesn't know the first thing about a house. These ladies don't who come back from foreign parts. Terrible mess there always was there to clean up, or so Mrs McGinty used to say. Yes, Monday afternoons and Thursday mornings Mrs Summerhayes, then Tuesday mornings Dr Rendell's and afternoons Mrs Upward at Laburnums. Wednesday was Mrs Wetherby at Hunter's Close and Friday Mrs Selkirk — Mrs Carpenter she is now. Mrs Upward's an elderly lady who lives with her son. They've got a maid, but she's getting on, and Mrs McGinty used to go once a week to give things a good turn out. Mr and Mrs Wetherby never seem to keep any help long — she's rather an invalid. Mr and Mrs Carpenter have a beautiful home and do a lot of entertaining. They're all very nice people.'

It was with this final pronouncement on the population of Broadhinny that Poirot went out into the street again.

He walked slowly up the hill towards Long

Meadows. He hoped devoutly that the contents of the bulged tin and the blood-stained beans had been duly eaten for lunch and had not been saved for a supper treat for him. But possibly there were other doubtful tins. Life at Long Meadows certainly had its dangers.

It had been, on the whole, a disappointing day.

What had he learned?

That James Bentley had a friend. That neither he nor Mrs McGinty had had any enemies. That Mrs McGinty had looked excited two days before her death and had bought a bottle of ink —

Poirot stopped dead . . . Was that a fact, a tiny fact at last?

He had asked idly, what Mrs McGinty should want with a bottle of ink, and Mrs Sweetiman had replied, quite seriously, that she supposed she wanted to write a letter.

There was significance there — a significance that had nearly escaped him because to him, as to most people, writing a letter was a common everyday occurrence.

But it was not so to Mrs McGinty. Writing a letter was to Mrs McGinty such an uncommon occurrence that she had to go out and buy a bottle of ink if she wanted to do so.

Mrs McGinty, then, hardly ever wrote

letters. Mrs Sweetiman, who was the postmistress, was thoroughly cognisant of the fact. But Mrs McGinty had written a letter two days before her death. To whom had she written and why?

It might be quite unimportant. She might have written to her niece — to an absent friend. Absurd to lay such stress on a simple thing like a bottle of ink.

But it was all he had got and he was going to follow it up.

A bottle of ink . . .

8

'A letter?' Bessie Burch shook her head. 'No, I didn't get any letter from auntie. What should she write to me about?'

Poirot suggested: 'There might have been something she wanted to tell you.'

'Auntie wasn't much of a one for writing. She was getting on for seventy, you know, and when she was young they didn't get much schooling.'

'But she could read and write?'

'Oh, of course. Not much of a one for reading, though she liked her *News of the World* and her *Sunday Comet*. But writing came a bit difficult always. If she'd anything to let me know about, like putting us off from coming to see her, or saying she couldn't come to us, she'd usually ring up Mr Benson, the chemist next door, and he'd send the message in. Very obliging that way, he is. You see, we're in the area, so it only costs twopence. There's a call-box at the post office in Broadhinny.'

Poirot nodded. He appreciated the fact that twopence was better than twopence ha'penny. He already had a picture of Mrs McGinty as the spare and saving kind. She had been, he thought, very fond of money.

He persisted gently:

'But your aunt did write to you sometimes, I suppose?'

'Well, there were cards at Christmas.'

'And perhaps she had friends in other parts of England to whom she wrote?'

'I don't know about that. There was her sister-in-law, but she died two years ago and there was a Mrs Birdlip — but she's dead too.'

'So, if she wrote to someone, it would be most likely in answer to a letter she had received?'

Again Bessie Burch looked doubtful.

'I don't know who'd be writing to her, I'm sure ... Of course,' her face brightened, 'there's always the Government.'

Poirot agreed that in these days, communications from what Bessie loosely referred to as 'the Government' were the rule, rather than the exception.

'And a lot of fandangle it usually is,' said Mrs Burch. 'Forms to fill in, and a lot of impertinent questions as shouldn't be asked of any decent body.'

'So Mrs McGinty might have got some Government communication that she had to answer?'

'If she had, she'd have brought it along to Joe, so as he could help her with it. Those sort of things fussed her and she always brought them to Joe.'

'Can you remember if there were any letters among her personal possessions?'

'I couldn't say rightly. I don't remember anything. But then the police took over at first. It wasn't for quite a while they let me pack her things and take them away.'

'What happened to those things?'

'That chest over there is hers — good solid mahogany, and there's a wardrobe upstairs, and some good kitchen stuff. The rest we sold because we'd no room for them.'

'I meant her own personal things.' He added: 'Such things as brushes and combs, photographs, toilet things, clothes . . . '

'Oh, them. Well, tell you the truth, I packed them in a suitcase and it's still upstairs. Didn't rightly know what to do with them. Thought I'd take the clothes to the jumble sale at Christmas, but I forgot. Didn't seem nice to take them to one of those nasty second-hand clothes people.'

'I wonder — might I see the contents of that suitcase?'

'Welcome, I'm sure. Though I don't think you'll find anything to help you. The police went through it all, you know.'

'Oh I know. But, all the same — '

Mrs Burch led him briskly into a minute back bedroom, used, Poirot judged, mainly for home dressmaking. She pulled out a suitcase from under the bed and said:

'Well, here you are, and you'll excuse me stopping, but I've got the stew to see to.'

Poirot gratefully excused her, and heard her thumping downstairs again. He drew the suitcase towards him and opened it.

A waft of mothballs came out to greet him.

With a feeling of pity, he lifted out the contents, so eloquent in their revelation of a woman who was dead. A rather worn long black coat. Two woollen jumpers. A coat and skirt. Stockings. No underwear (presumably Bessie Burch had taken those for her own wear). Two pairs of shoes wrapped up in newspaper. A brush and comb, worn but clean. An old dented silver-backed mirror. A photograph in a leather frame of a wedding pair dressed in the style of thirty years ago — a picture of Mrs McGinty and her husband presumably. Two picture post-cards of Margate. A china dog. A recipe torn out of a paper for making vegetable marrow jam. Another piece dealing with 'Flying Saucers' on a sensational note. A third clipping dealt with Mother Shipton's prophecies. There was also a Bible and a Prayer Book.

There were no handbags, or gloves. Presumably Bessie Burch had taken these, or given them away. The clothes here, Poirot judged, would have been too small for the buxom Bessie. Mrs McGinty had been a thin, spare woman.

He unwrapped one of the pairs of shoes. They were of quite good quality and not much worn. Decidedly on the small side for Bessie Burch.

He was just about to wrap them up neatly again when his eye was caught by the heading on the piece of newspaper.

It was the *Sunday Comet* and the date was November 19th.

Mrs McGinty had been killed on November 22nd.

This then was the paper she had bought on the Sunday preceding her death. It had been lying in her room and Bessie Burch had used it in due course to wrap up her aunt's things.

Sunday, November 19th. And on *Monday* Mrs McGinty had gone into the post office to buy a bottle of ink . . .

Could that be because of something she had seen in Sunday's newspaper?

He unwrapped the other pair of shoes. They were wrapped in the *News of the World* of the same date.

He smoothed out both papers and took them over to a chair where he sat down to read them. And at once he made a discovery. On one page of the *Sunday Comet*, something had been cut out. It was a rectangular piece out of the middle page. The space was too big for any of the clippings he had found.

He looked through both newspapers, but could find nothing else of interest. He wrapped them round the shoes again and packed the suitcase tidily.

Then he went downstairs.

Mrs Burch was busy in the kitchen.

'Don't suppose you found anything?' she said.

'Alas, no.' He added in a casual voice: 'You do not remember if there was a cutting from a newspaper in your aunt's purse or in her handbag, was there?'

'Can't remember any. Perhaps the police took it.'

But the police had not taken it. That Poirot knew from his study of Spence's notes. The contents of the dead woman's handbag had been listed, no newspaper cutting was among them.

'*Eh bien*,' said Hercule Poirot to himself. 'The next step is easy. It will be either the wash-out — or else, at last, I advance.'

II

Sitting very still, with the dusty files of newspaper in front of him, Poirot told himself that his recognition of the significance of the bottle of ink had not played him false.

The *Sunday Comet* was given to romantic dramatizations of past events.

The paper at which Poirot was looking was the *Sunday Comet* of Sunday, November 19th.

At the top of the middle page were these words in big type:

WOMEN VICTIMS OF
BYGONE TRAGEDIES
WHERE ARE THESE
WOMEN NOW?

Below the caption were four very blurred reproductions of photographs clearly taken many years ago.

The subjects of them did not look tragic. They looked, actually, rather ridiculous, since nearly all of them were dressed in the style of a bygone day, and nothing is more ridiculous than the fashions of yesterday — though in another thirty years or so their charm may have reappeared, or at any rate be once more apparent.

Under each photo was a name.

Eva Kane, the 'other woman' in the famous Craig Case.

Janice Courtland, the 'tragic wife' whose husband was a fiend in human form.

Little Lily Gamboll, tragic child product of our overcrowded age.

Vera Blake, unsuspecting wife of a killer.

And then came the question in bold type again:

WHERE ARE THESE WOMEN NOW?

Poirot blinked and set himself to read meticulously the somewhat romantic prose which gave the life stories of these dim and blurry heroines.

The name of Eva Kane he remembered, for the Craig Case had been a very celebrated one. Alfred Craig had been Town Clerk of Parminster, a conscientious, rather nondescript little man, correct and pleasant in his behaviour. He had had the misfortune to marry a tiresome and temperamental wife. Mrs Craig ran him into debt, bullied him, nagged him, and suffered from nervous maladies that unkind friends said were entirely imaginary. Eva Kane was the young nursery governess in the house. She was nineteen, pretty, helpless and rather simple. She fell desperately in love with Craig and he with her. Then one day the neighbours heard that Mrs Craig had been 'ordered abroad' for her health. That had been Craig's story. He took her up to London, the first stage of the journey, by car late one evening, and 'saw her off' to the South of France. Then he returned to Parminster and at intervals mentioned how his wife's health was no better by her accounts of it in letters. Eva Kane remained behind to housekeep for him, and tongues soon started wagging. Finally, Craig received news of his wife's death abroad. He went away and returned a week later, with an account of the funeral.

In some ways, Craig was a simple man. He made the mistake of mentioning where his wife had died, a moderately well-known resort on the French Riviera. It only remained for someone who had a relative or friend living there to write to them, discover that there had been no death or funeral of anyone of that name and, after a period of rank gossip, to communicate with the police.

Subsequent events can be briefly summarized.

Mrs Craig had not left for the Riviera. She had been cut in neat pieces and buried in the Craig cellar. And the autopsy of the remains showed poisoning by a vegetable alkaloid.

Craig was arrested and sent for trial. Eva Kane was originally charged as an accessory, but the charge was dropped, since it appeared clear that she had throughout been completely ignorant of what had occurred. Craig in the end made a full confession and was sentenced and executed.

Eva Kane, who was expecting a child, left Parminster and, in the words of the *Sunday Comet:*

Kindly relatives in the New World offered her a home. Changing her name, the pitiful young girl, seduced in her trusting youth by a cold-blooded murderer, left these shores for ever, to begin a new life and to keep for ever locked in her heart and concealed from her daughter the name of her father.

'My daughter shall grow up happy and innocent. Her life shall not be

tainted by the cruel past. That I have sworn. My tragic memories shall remain mine alone.'

Poor frail trusting Eva Kane. To learn, so young, the villainy and infamy of man. Where is she now? Is there, in some Mid-western town, an elderly woman, quiet and respected by her neighbours, who has, perhaps, sad eyes . . . And does a young woman, happy and cheerful, with children, perhaps, of her own, come and see 'Momma', telling her of all the little rubs and grievances of daily life — with no idea of what past sufferings her mother has endured?

'Oh la la!' said Hercule Poirot. And passed on to the next Tragic Victim.

Janice Courtland, the 'tragic wife', had certainly been unfortunate in her husband. His peculiar practices referred to in such a guarded way as to rouse instant curiosity, had been suffered by her for eight years. Eight years of martyrdom, the *Sunday Comet* said firmly. Then Janice made a friend. An idealistic and unworldly young man who, horrified by a scene between husband and wife that he had witnessed by accident, had thereupon assaulted the husband with such vigour that the latter had crashed in his skull on a sharply-edged marble fire surround. The jury had found that provocation had been intense, that the young idealist had had no intention of killing, and a sentence of five years for manslaughter was given.

The suffering Janice, horrified by all the publicity the case had brought her, had gone abroad 'to forget'.

Has she forgotten? asked the *Sunday Comet. We hope so. Somewhere, perhaps, is a happy wife and mother to whom those years of nightmare suffering silently endured, seem now only like a dream . . .*

'Well, well,' said Hercule Poirot and passed on to Lily Gamboll, the tragic child product of our overcrowded age.

Lily Gamboll had, it seemed, been removed from her overcrowded home. An aunt had assumed responsibility for Lily's life. Lily had wanted to go to the pictures, aunt had said 'No.' Lily Gamboll had picked up the meat chopper which was lying conveniently on the table and had aimed a blow at her aunt with it. The aunt, though autocratic, was small and frail. The blow killed her. Lily was a well-developed and muscular child for her twelve years. An approved school had opened its doors and Lily had disappeared from the everyday scene.

By now she is a woman, free again to take her place in our civilization. Her conduct, during her years of confinement and probation, is said to have been exemplary. Does not this show that it is not the child, but the system, that we must blame? Brought up in ignorance, little Lily was the victim of her environment.

Now, having atoned for her tragic lapse, she lives somewhere, happily, we hope, a good citizen and a good wife and mother. Poor little Lily Gamboll.

Poirot shook his head. A child of twelve who took a swing at her aunt with a meat chopper and hit her hard enough to kill her was not, in his opinion, a nice child. His sympathies were, in this case, with the aunt.

He passed on to Vera Blake.

Vera Blake was clearly one of those women with whom everything goes wrong. She had first taken up with a boyfriend who turned out to be a gangster wanted by the police for killing a bank watchman. She had then married a respectable tradesman who turned out to be a receiver of stolen goods. Her two children had likewise, in due course, attracted the attention of the police. They went with Mamma to department stores and did a pretty line in shoplifting. Finally, however, a 'good man' had appeared on the scene. He had offered tragic Vera a home in the Dominions. She and her children should leave this effete country.

From henceforward a New Life awaited them. At last, after long years of repeated blows from Fate, Vera's troubles are over.

'I wonder,' said Poirot sceptically. 'Very possibly she will find she has married a confidence trickster who works the liners!'

He leant back and studied the four photographs. Eva Kane with tousled curly hair over her ears and an enormous hat, held a bunch of roses up to her ear like a telephone receiver. Janice Courtland had a cloche hat pushed down over her ears and a waist round her hips. Lily Gamboll was a plain child with an adenoidal appearance of open mouth, hard breathing and thick spectacles. Vera Blake was so tragically black and white that no features showed.

For some reason Mrs McGinty had torn out this feature, photographs and all. Why? Just to keep because the stories interested her? He thought not. Mrs McGinty had kept very few things during her sixty-odd years of life. Poirot knew that from the police reports of her belongings.

She had torn this out on the Sunday and on the Monday she had bought a bottle of ink and the inference was that she, who never wrote letters, was about to write a letter. If it had been a business letter, she would probably have asked Joe Burch to help her. So it had not been business. It had been — what?

Poirot's eyes looked over the four photographs once again.

Where, the *Sunday Comet* asked, *are these women now?*

One of them, Poirot thought, might have been in Broadhinny last November.

III

It was not until the following day that Poirot found himself tête-à-tête with Miss Pamela Horsefall.

95

Miss Horsefall couldn't give him long, because she had to rush away to Sheffield, she explained.

Miss Horsefall was tall, manly-looking, a hard drinker and smoker, and it would seem, looking at her, highly improbable that it was her pen which had dropped such treacly sentiment in the *Sunday Comet*. Nevertheless it was so.

'Cough it up, cough it up,' said Miss Horsefall impatiently to Poirot. 'I've got to be going.'

'It is about your article in the *Sunday Comet*. Last November. The series about Tragic Women.'

'Oh, *that* series. Pretty lousy, weren't they?'

Poirot did not express an opinion on that point. He said:

'I refer in particular to the article on Women Associated with Crime that appeared on November 19th. It concerned Eva Kane, Vera Blake, Janice Courtland and Lily Gamboll.'

Miss Horsefall grinned.

'*Where are these tragic women now?* I remember.'

'I suppose you sometimes get letters after the appearance of these articles?'

'You bet I do! Some people seem to have nothing better to do than write letters.

Somebody 'once saw the murderer Craig walking down the street'. Somebody would like to tell me 'the story of her life, far more tragic than anything I could ever imagine'. '

'Did you get a letter after the appearance of that article from a Mrs McGinty of Broadhinny?'

'My dear man, how on earth should I know? I get buckets of letters. How should I remember one particular name?'

'I thought you might remember,' said Poirot, 'because a few days later Mrs McGinty was murdered.'

'Now you're talking.' Miss Horsefall forgot to be impatient to get to Sheffield, and sat down astride a chair. 'McGinty — McGinty . . . I do remember the name. Conked on the head by her lodger. Not a very exciting crime from the point of view of the public. No sex appeal about it. You say the woman wrote to me?'

'She wrote to the *Sunday Comet*, I think.'

'Same thing. It would come on to me. And with the murder — and her name being in the news — surely I should remember — ' she stopped. 'Look here — it wasn't from Broadhinny. It was from Broadway.'

'So you do remember?'

'Well, I'm not sure . . . But the name . . . Comic name, isn't it? McGinty! Yes

— atrocious writing and quite illiterate. If I'd only realized . . . But I'm sure it came from Broadway.'

Poirot said: 'You say yourself the writing was bad. Broadway and Broadhinny — they could look alike.'

'Yes — might be so. After all, one wouldn't be likely to know these queer rural names. McGinty — yes. I do remember definitely. Perhaps the murder fixed the name for me.'

'Can you remember what she said in her letter?'

'Something about a photograph. She knew where there was a photograph like in the paper — and would we pay her anything for it and how much?'

'And you answered?'

'My dear man, we don't want anything of that kind. We sent back the standard reply. Polite thanks but nothing doing. But as we sent it to Broadway — I don't suppose she'd ever get it.'

'*She knew where there was a photograph . . .* '

Into Poirot's mind there came back a remembrance. Maureen Summerhayes' careless voice saying, 'Of course she snooped round a bit.'

Mrs McGinty had snooped. She was honest, but she liked to know about things.

And people kept things — foolish, meaningless things from the past. Kept them for sentimental reasons, or just overlooked them and didn't remember they were there.

Mrs McGinty had seen an old photograph and later she had recognized it reproduced in the *Sunday Comet*. And she had wondered if there was any money in it . . .

He rose briskly. 'Thank you, Miss Horsefall. You will pardon me, but those notes on the cases that you wrote, were they accurate? I notice, for instance, that the year of the Craig trial is given wrongly — it was actually a year later than you say. And in the Courtland case, the husband's name was Herbert, I seem to remember, not Hubert. Lily Gamboll's aunt lived in Buckinghamshire, not Berkshire.'

Miss Horsefall waved a cigarette.

'My dear man. No point in accuracy. Whole thing was a romantic farrago from beginning to end. I just mugged up the facts a bit and then let fly with a lot of hou ha.'

'What I am trying to say is that even the characters of your heroines are not, perhaps, quite as represented.'

Pamela let out a neighing sound like a horse.

''Course they weren't. What do *you* think? I've no doubt that Eva Kane was a thorough little bitch, and not an injured innocent at all. And as for the Courtland woman, why did she suffer in silence for eight years with a sadistic pervert? Because he was rolling in money, and the romantic boy-friend hadn't any.'

'And the tragic child, Lily Gamboll?'

'I wouldn't care to have her gambolling about *me* with a meat chopper.'

Poirot ticked off on his fingers.

'They left the country — they went to the New World — abroad — 'to the Dominions' — 'to start a New Life.' And there is nothing to show, is there, that they did not, subsequently, come back to this country?'

'Not a thing,' agreed Miss Horsefall. 'And now — I really must fly — '

Later that night Poirot rang up Spence.

'I've been wondering about you, Poirot. Have you got anything? Anything at all?'

'I have made my inquiries,' said Poirot grimly.

'Yes?'

'And the result of them is this: *The people who live in Broadhinny are all very nice people.*'

'What do you mean by that, M. Poirot?'

'Oh, my friend, consider. 'Very nice people.' That has been, before now, a motive for murder.'

9

I

'All very nice people,' murmured Poirot as he turned in at the gate of Crossways, near the station.

A brass plate in the doorpost announced that Dr Rendell, M.D., lived there.

Dr Rendell was a large cheerful man of forty. He greeted his guest with definite *empressement*.

'Our quiet little village is honoured,' he said, 'by the presence of the great Hercule Poirot.'

'Ah,' said Poirot. He was gratified. 'You have, then, heard of me?'

'Of course we have heard of you. Who hasn't?'

The answer to that would have been damaging to Poirot's self-esteem. He merely said politely: 'I am fortunate to find you at home.'

It was not particularly fortunate. It was, on the contrary, astute timing. But Dr Rendell replied heartily:

'Yes. Just caught me. Surgery in a quarter of an hour. Now what can I do for you? I'm devoured with curiosity to know what you're doing down here. A rest cure? Or have we crime in our midst?'

'In the past tense — not the present.'

'Past? I don't remember — '

'Mrs McGinty.'

'Of course. Of course. I was forgetting. But don't say you're concerned with that — at this late date?'

'If I may mention this to you in confidence, I am employed by the defence. Fresh evidence on which to lodge an appeal.'

Dr Rendell said sharply: 'But what fresh evidence can there be?'

'That, alas, I am not at liberty to state — '

'Oh, quite — please forgive me.'

'But I have come across certain things which are, I may say — very curious — very — how shall I put it? — suggestive? I came to you, Dr Rendell, because I understand that Mrs McGinty occasionally was employed here.'

'Oh yes, yes — she was — What about a drink? Sherry? Whisky? You prefer sherry? So do I.' He brought two glasses and, sitting down by Poirot, he went on: 'She used to come once a week to do extra cleaning. I've got a very good housekeeper — excellent

— but the brasses — and scrubbing the kitchen floor — well, my Mrs Scott can't get down on her knees very well. Mrs McGinty was an excellent worker.'

'Do you think that she was a truthful person?'

'Truthful? Well, that's an odd question. I don't think I could say — no opportunity of knowing. As far as I know she was quite truthful.'

'If then she made a statement to anyone, you think that statement would probably be true?'

Dr Rendell looked faintly disturbed.

'Oh, I wouldn't like to go as far as that. I really know so little about her. I could ask Mrs Scott. She'd know better.'

'No, no. It would be better not to do that.'

'You're arousing my curiosity,' said Dr Rendell genially. 'What was it she was going around saying? Something a bit libellous, was it? Slanderous, I suppose I mean.'

Poirot merely shook his head. He said: 'You understand, all this is extremely hush hush at present. I am only at the very commencement of my investigation.'

Dr Rendell said rather drily:

'You'll have to hurry a bit, won't you?'

'You are right. The time at my disposal is short.'

'I must say you surprise me . . . We've all been quite sure down here that Bentley did it. There didn't seem any doubt possible.'

'It seemed an ordinary sordid crime — not very interesting. That is what you would say?'

'Yes — yes, that sums it up very fairly.'

'You knew James Bentley?'

'He came to see me professionally once or twice. He was nervous about his own health. Coddled by his mother, I fancy. One sees that so often. We've another case in point here.'

'Ah, indeed?'

'Yes. Mrs Upward. Laura Upward. Dotes upon that son of hers. She keeps him well tied to her apronstrings. He's a clever fellow — not quite as clever as he thinks himself, between you and me — but still definitely talented. By way of being a budding playwright is our Robin.'

'They have been here long?'

'Three or four years. Nobody has been in Broadhinny very long. The original village was only a handful of cottages, grouped round Long Meadows. You're staying there, I understand?'

'I am,' said Poirot without undue elation.

Dr Rendell appeared amused.

'Guest House indeed,' he said. 'What that young woman knows about running a Guest House is just nothing at all. She's lived in

India all her married life with servants running round all over the place. I bet you're uncomfortable. Nobody ever stays long. As for poor old Summerhayes, he'll never make anything of this market gardening stunt he's trying to run. Nice fellow — but not an idea of the commercial life — and the commercial life it's got to be nowadays if you want to keep your head above water. Don't run away with the idea that I heal the sick. I'm just a glorified form-filler and signer of certificates. I like the Summerhayes, though. She's a charming creature, and though Summerhayes has a devilish temper and is inclined to be moody, he's one of the old gang. Out of the top drawer all right. You should have known old Colonel Summerhayes, a regular tartar, proud as the devil.'

'That was Major Summerhayes' father?'

'Yes. There wasn't much money when the old boy died and of course there have been death duties to cripple these people, but they're determined to stick to the old place. One doesn't know whether to admire them, or whether to say 'Silly fools.' '

He looked at his watch.

'I must not keep you,' said Poirot.

'I've got a few minutes still. Besides, I'd like you to meet my wife. I can't think where she is. She was immensely interested to hear you were down here. We're both very crime-minded. Read a lot about it.'

'Criminology, fiction, or the Sunday papers?' asked Poirot smiling.

'All three.'

'Do you descend as low as the *Sunday Comet*?'

Rendell laughed.

'What would Sunday be without it?'

'They had some interesting articles about five months ago. One in particular about women who had been involved in murder cases and the tragedy of their lives.'

'Yes, I remember the one you mean. All a lot of hooey, though.'

'Ah, you think that?'

'Well of course the Craig case I only know from reading about it, but one of the others — Courtland case, I can tell you *that* woman was no tragic innocent. Regular vicious bit of goods. I know because an uncle of mine attended the husband. He was certainly no beauty, but his wife wasn't much better. She got hold of that young greenhorn and egged him on to murder. Then he goes to prison for manslaughter and she goes off, a rich widow, and marries someone else.'

'The *Sunday Comet* did not mention that. Do you remember whom she married?'

Rendell shook his head.

'Don't think I ever heard the name, but someone told me that she'd done pretty well for herself.'

'One wondered in reading the article where those four women were now,' mused Poirot.

'I know. One may have met one of them at a party last week. I bet they all keep their past pretty dark. You'd certainly never recognize any of 'em from those photographs. My word, they looked a plain lot.'

The clock chimed and Poirot rose to his feet. 'I must detain you no longer. You have been most kind.'

'Not much help, I'm afraid. The mere man barely knows what his charlady looks like. But half a second, you must meet the wife. She'd never forgive me.'

He preceded Poirot out into the hall, calling loudly:

'Shelagh — Shelagh — '

A faint answer came from upstairs.

'Come down here. I've got something for you.'

A thin fair-haired pale woman ran lightly down the stairs.

'Here's M. Hercule Poirot, Shelagh. What do you think of that?'

'Oh,' Mrs Rendell appeared to be startled out of speaking. Her very pale blue eyes stared at Poirot apprehensively.

'Madame,' said Poirot, bowing over her head in his most foreign manner.

'We heard that you were here,' said Shelagh Rendell. 'But we didn't know — ' She broke off. Her light eyes went quickly to her husband's face.

'It is from him she takes the Greenwich time,' said Poirot to himself.

He uttered a few florid phrases and took his leave.

An impression remained with him of a genial Dr Rendell and a tongue-tied, apprehensive Mrs Rendell.

So much for the Rendells, where Mrs McGinty had gone to work on Tuesday mornings.

II

Hunter's Close was a solidly built Victorian house approached by a long untidy drive overgrown with weeds. It had not originally been considered a big house, but was now big enough to be inconvenient domestically.

Poirot inquired of the foreign young woman who opened the door for Mrs Wetherby.

She stared at him and then said: 'I do not know. Please to come. Miss Henderson perhaps?'

108

She left him standing in the hall. It was in an estate agent's phrase 'fully furnished' — with a good many curios from various parts of the world. Nothing looked very clean or well dusted.

Presently the foreign girl reappeared. She said: 'Please to come,' and showed him into a chilly little room with a large desk. On the mantelpiece was a big and rather evil-looking copper coffee pot with an enormous hooked spout like a large hooked nose.

The door opened behind Poirot and a girl came into the room.

'My mother is lying down,' she said. 'Can I do anything for you?'

'You are Miss Wetherby?'

'Henderson. Mr Wetherby is my stepfather.'

She was a plain girl of about thirty, large and awkward. She had watchful eyes.

'I was anxious to hear what you could tell me about Mrs McGinty who used to work here.'

She stared at him.

'Mrs McGinty? But she's dead.'

'I know that,' said Poirot gently. 'Nevertheless, I would like to hear about her.'

'Oh. Is it for insurance or something?'

'Not for insurance. It is a question of fresh evidence.'

'Fresh evidence. You mean — her death?'

'I am engaged,' said Poirot, 'by the solicitors for the defence to make an inquiry on James Bentley's behalf.'

Staring at him, she asked: 'But didn't he do it?'

'The jury thought he did. But juries have been known to make a mistake.'

'Then it was really someone else who killed her?'

'It may have been.'

She asked abruptly: 'Who?'

'That,' said Poirot softly, 'is the question.'

'I don't understand at all.'

'No? But you can tell me something about Mrs McGinty, can't you?'

She said rather reluctantly:

'I suppose so . . . What do you want to know?'

'Well — to begin with — what did you think of her?'

'Why — nothing in particular. She was just like anybody else.'

'Talkative or silent? Curious or reserved? Pleasant or morose? A nice woman, or — not a very nice woman?'

Miss Henderson reflected.

'She worked well — but she talked a lot. Sometimes she said rather funny things . . . I didn't — really — like her very much.'

The door opened and the foreign help said:

'Miss Deirdre, your mother say: please to bring.'

'My mother wants me to take this gentleman upstairs to her?'

'Yes please, thank you.'

Deirdre Henderson looked at Poirot doubtfully.

'Will you come up to my mother?'

'But certainly.'

Deirdre led the way across the hall and up the stairs. She said inconsequently: 'One does get so very tired of foreigners.'

Since her mind was clearly running on her domestic help and not on the visitor, Poirot did not take offence. He reflected that Deirdre Henderson seemed a rather simple young woman — simple to the point of gaucheness.

The room upstairs was crowded with knick-knacks. It was the room of a woman who had travelled a good deal and who had been determined wherever she went to have a souvenir of the place. Most of the souvenirs were clearly made for the delight and exploitation of tourists. There were too many sofas and tables and chairs in the room, too little air and too many draperies — and in the midst of it all was Mrs Wetherby.

Mrs Wetherby seemed a small woman — a pathetic small woman in a large room. That was the effect. But she was not really quite so small as she had decided to appear. The 'poor little me' type can achieve its result quite well, even if really of medium height.

She was reclining very comfortably on a sofa and near her were books and some knitting and a glass of orange juice and a box of chocolates. She said brightly:

'You *must* forgive me not getting up, but the doctor does so insist on my resting every day, and everyone scolds me if I don't do what I'm told.'

Poirot took her extended hand and bowed over it with the proper murmur of homage.

Behind him, uncompromising, Deirdre said: 'He wants to know about Mrs McGinty.'

The delicate hand that had lain passively in his tightened and he was reminded for a moment of the talon of a bird. Not really a piece of delicate Dresden china — a scratchy predatory claw . . .

Laughing slightly, Mrs Wetherby said:

'How ridiculous you are, Deirdre darling. Who is Mrs McGinty?'

'Oh, Mummy — you do remember really. She worked for us. You know, the one who was murdered.'

Mrs Wetherby closed her eyes, and shivered.

'Don't, darling. It was all so horrid. I felt

nervous for weeks afterwards. Poor old woman, but so *stupid* to keep money under the floor. She ought to have put it in the bank. Of course I remember all that — I'd just forgotten her *name*.'

Deirdre said stolidly:

'He wants to know about her.'

'Now do sit down, M. Poirot. I'm quite devoured by curiosity. Mrs Rendell just rang up and she said we had a very famous criminologist down here, and she described you. And then, when that idiot Frieda described a visitor, I felt sure it must be you, and I sent down word for you to come up. Now tell me, what *is* all this?'

'It is as your daughter says, I want to know about Mrs McGinty. She worked here. She came to you, I understand, on Wednesdays. And it was on a Wednesday she died. So she had been here that day, had she not?'

'I suppose so. Yes, I suppose so. I can't really tell now. It's so long ago.'

'Yes. Several months. And she did not say anything that day — anything special?'

'That class of person always talks a lot,' said Mrs Wetherby with distaste. 'One doesn't really listen. And anyway, she couldn't tell she was going to be robbed and killed that night, could she?'

'There is cause and effect,' said Poirot.

Mrs Wetherby wrinkled her forehead.

'I don't see what you mean.'

'Perhaps I do not see myself — not yet. One works through darkness towards light . . . Do you take in the Sunday papers, Mrs Wetherby?'

Her blue eyes opened very wide.

'Oh yes. Of course. We have the *Observer* and the *Sunday Times*. Why?'

'I wondered. Mrs McGinty took the *Sunday Comet* and the *News of the World*.'

He paused but nobody said anything. Mrs Wetherby sighed and half closed her eyes. She said:

'It was all very upsetting. That horrible lodger of hers. I don't think really he can have been quite right in the head. Apparently he was quite an educated man, too. That makes it worse, doesn't it?'

'Does it?'

'Oh yes — I do think so. Such a brutal crime. A meat chopper. Ugh!'

'The police never found the weapon,' said Poirot.

'I expect he threw it in a pond or something.'

'They dragged the ponds,' said Deirdre. 'I saw them.'

'Darling,' her mother sighed, 'don't be morbid. You know how I hate thinking of things like that. My head.'

Fiercely the girl turned on Poirot.

'You mustn't go on about it,' she said. 'It's bad for her. She's frightfully sensitive. She can't even read detective stories.'

'My apologies,' said Poirot. He rose to his feet. 'I have only one excuse. A man is to be hanged in three weeks' time. If he did not do it — '

Mrs Wetherby raised herself on her elbow. Her voice was shrill.

'But of course he did it,' she cried. 'Of course he did.'

Poirot shook his head.

'I am not so sure.'

He left the room quickly. As he went down the stairs, the girl came after him. She caught up with him in the hall.

'What do you mean?' she asked.

'What I said, mademoiselle.'

'Yes, but — ' She stopped.

Poirot said nothing.

Deirdre Henderson said slowly:

'You've upset my mother. She hates things like that — robberies and murders and — and violence.'

'It must, then, have been a great shock to her when a woman who had actually worked here was killed.'

'Oh yes — oh yes, it was.'

'She was prostrated — yes?'

'She wouldn't hear anything about it . . . We — I — we try to — to spare her things. All the beastliness.'

'What about the war?'

'Luckily we never had any bombs near here.'

'What was your part in the war, mademoiselle?'

'Oh, I did VAD work in Kilchester. And some driving for the WVS I couldn't have left home, of course. Mother needed me. As it was, she minded my being out so much. It was all very difficult. And then servants — naturally mother's never done any housework — she's not strong enough. And it was so difficult to get anyone at all. That's why Mrs McGinty was such a blessing. That's when she began coming to us. She was a splendid worker. But of course nothing — anywhere — is like it used to be.'

'And do you mind that so much, mademoiselle?'

'I? Oh no.' She seemed surprised. 'But it's different for mother. She — she lives in the past a lot.'

'Some people do,' said Poirot. His visual memory conjured up the room he had been in a short time before. There had been a bureau drawer half pulled out. A drawer full of odds and ends — a silk pin-cushion, a broken fan, a silver coffee pot — some old magazines. The drawer had been too full to shut. He said softly: 'And they keep things — memories of old days — the dance programme, the fan, the photographs of bygone friends, even the menu cards and the theatre programmes because, looking at these things, old memories revive.'

'I suppose that's it,' said Deirdre. 'I can't understand it myself. I never keep anything.'

'You look forwards, not back?'

Deirdre said slowly:

'I don't know that I look anywhere . . . I mean, today's usually enough, isn't it?'

The front door opened and a tall, spare, elderly man came into the hall. He stopped dead as he saw Poirot.

He glanced at Deirdre and his eyebrows rose in interrogation.

'This is my stepfather,' said Deirdre. 'I — I don't know your name?'

'I am Hercule Poirot,' said Poirot with his usual embarrassed air of announcing a royal title.

Mr Wetherby seemed unimpressed.

He said, 'Ah,' and turned to hang up his coat.

Deirdre said:

'He came to ask about Mrs McGinty.'

Mr Wetherby remained still for a second, then he finished his adjustment of the coat on the peg.

'That seems to me rather remarkable,' he said. 'The woman met her death some months ago and, although she worked here, we have no information concerning her or her family. If we had done we should already have given it to the police.'

There was finality in his tone. He glanced at his watch.

'Lunch, I presume, will be ready in a quarter of an hour.'

'I'm afraid it may be rather late today.'

Mr Wetherby's eyebrows rose again.

'Indeed? Why, may I ask?'

'Frieda has been rather busy.'

'My dear Deirdre, I hate to remind you, but the task of running the household devolves on you. I should appreciate a little more punctuality.'

Poirot opened the front door and let himself out. He glanced over his shoulder.

There was cold dislike in the gaze that Mr Wetherby gave his stepdaughter. There was something very like hate in the eyes that looked back at him.

10

Poirot left his third call until after luncheon. Luncheon was under-stewed oxtail, watery potatoes, and what Maureen hoped optimistically might turn out to be pancakes. They were very peculiar.

Poirot walked slowly up the hill. Presently, on his right, he would come to Laburnums, two cottages knocked into one and remodelled to modern taste. Here lived Mrs Upward and that promising young playwright, Robin Upward.

Poirot paused a moment at the gate to pass a hand over his moustaches. As he did so a car came twisting slowly down the hill and an apple core directed with force struck him on the cheek.

Startled, Poirot let out a yelp of protest. The car halted and a head came through the window.

'I'm so sorry. Did I hit you?'

Poirot paused in the act of replying. He looked at the rather noble face, the massive brow, the untidy billows of grey hair and a chord of memory stirred. The apple core, too, assisted his memory.

'But surely,' he exclaimed, 'it is Mrs Oliver.'

It was indeed that celebrated detective-story writer.

Exclaiming, 'Why, it's M. Poirot,' the authoress attempted to extract herself from the car. It was a small car and Mrs Oliver was a large woman. Poirot hastened to assist.

Murmuring in an explanatory voice, 'Stiff after the long drive,' Mrs Oliver suddenly arrived out on the road, rather in the manner of a volcanic eruption.

Large quantities of apples came, too, and rolled merrily down the hill.

'Bag's burst,' explained Mrs Oliver.

She brushed a few stray pieces of half-consumed apple from the jutting shelf of her bust and then shook herself rather like a large Newfoundland dog. The last apple, concealed in the recesses of her person, joined its brothers and sisters.

'Pity the bag burst,' said Mrs Oliver. 'They were Cox's. Still I suppose there will be lots of apples down here in the country. Or aren't there? Perhaps they all get sent away. Things are so odd nowadays, I find. Well, how are you, M. Poirot? You don't live here, do you? No, I'm sure you don't. Then I suppose it's murder? Not my hostess, I hope?'

'Who is your hostess?'

'In there,' said Mrs Oliver, nodding her

head. 'That's to say if that's a house called Laburnums, half-way down the hill on the left side after you pass the church. Yes, that must be it. What's she like?'

'You do not know her?'

'No, I've come down professionally, so to speak. A book of mine is being dramatized — by Robin Upward. We're supposed to sort of get together over it.'

'My felicitations, madame.'

'It's not like that at all,' said Mrs Oliver. 'So far it's pure *agony*. Why I ever let myself in for it I don't know. My books bring me in quite enough money — that is to say the bloodsuckers take most of it, and if I made more, they'd take more, so I don't overstrain myself. But you've no idea of the agony of having your characters taken and made to say things that they never would have said, and do things that they never would have done. And if you protest, all they say is that it's 'good theatre'. That's all Robin Upward thinks of. Everyone says he's very clever. If he's so clever I don't see why he doesn't write a play of his own and leave my poor unfortunate Finn alone. He's not even a Finn any longer. He's become a member of the Norwegian Resistance Movement.' She ran her hands through her hair. 'What have I done with my hat?'

Poirot looked into the car.

'I think, madame, that you must have been sitting on it.'

'It does look like it,' agreed Mrs Oliver, surveying the wreckage. 'Oh well,' she continued cheerfully, 'I never liked it much. But I thought I might have to go to church on Sunday, and although the Archbishop has said one needn't, I still think that the more old-fashioned clergy expect one to wear a hat. But tell me about your murder or whatever it is. Do you remember *our* murder?'

'Very well indeed.'

'Rather fun, wasn't it? Not the actual murder — I didn't like that at all. But afterwards. Who is it this time?'

'Not so picturesque a person as Mr Shaitana. An elderly charwoman who was robbed and murdered five months ago. You may have read about it. Mrs McGinty. A young man was convicted and sentenced to death — '

'And he didn't do it, but you know who did, and you're going to prove it,' said Mrs Oliver rapidly. 'Splendid.'

'You go too fast,' said Poirot with a sigh. 'I do not yet know who did it — and from there it will be a long way to prove it.'

'Men are so slow,' said Mrs Oliver disparagingly. 'I'll soon tell you who did it.

Someone down here, I suppose? Give me a day or two to look round, and I'll spot the murderer. A woman's intuition — that's what you need. I was quite right over the Shaitana case, wasn't I?'

Poirot gallantly forbode to remind Mrs Oliver of her rapid changes of suspicion on that occasion.

'You men,' said Mrs Oliver indulgently. 'Now if a woman were the head of Scotland Yard — '

She left this well-worn theme hanging in the air as a voice hailed them from the door of the cottage.

'Hallo,' said the voice, an agreeable light tenor. 'Is that Mrs Oliver?'

'Here I am,' called Mrs Oliver. To Poirot she murmured: 'Don't worry. I'll be very discreet.'

'No, no, madame. I do not want you to be discreet. *On the contrary.*'

Robin Upward came down the path and through the gate. He was bareheaded and wore very old grey flannel trousers and a disreputable sports coat. But for a tendency to embonpoint, he would have been good looking.

'Ariadne, my precious!' he exclaimed and embraced her warmly.

He stood away, his hands on her shoulders.

'My dear, I've had the most marvellous idea for the second act.'

'Have you?' said Mrs Oliver without enthusiasm. 'This is M. Hercule Poirot.'

'Splendid,' said Robin. 'Have you got any luggage?'

'Yes, it's in the back.'

Robin hauled out a couple of suitcases.

'Such a bore,' he said. 'We've no proper servants. Only old Janet. And we have to spare her all the time. That's such a nuisance don't you think? How heavy your cases are. Have you got bombs in them?'

He staggered up the path, calling out over his shoulder:

'Come in and have a drink.'

'He means you,' said Mrs Oliver, removing her handbag, a book, and a pair of old shoes from the front seat. 'Did you actually say just now that you wanted me to be *indiscreet?*'

'The more indiscreet the better.'

'I shouldn't tackle it that way myself,' said Mrs Oliver, 'but it's *your* murder. I'll help all I can.'

Robin reappeared at the front door.

'Come in, come in,' he called. 'We'll see about the car later. Madre is dying to meet you.'

Mrs Oliver swept up the path and Hercule Poirot followed her.

The interior of Laburnums was charming. Poirot guessed that a very large sum of money had been spent on it, but the result was an expensive and charming simplicity. Each small piece of cottage oak was a genuine piece.

In a wheeled chair by the fireplace of the living-room Laura Upward smiled a welcome. She was a vigorous looking woman of sixty-odd, with iron-grey hair and a determined chin.

'I'm delighted to meet you, Mrs Oliver,' she said. 'I expect you hate people talking to you about your books, but they've been an enormous solace to me for years — and especially since I've been such a cripple.'

'That's very nice of you,' said Mrs Oliver, looking uncomfortable and twisting her hands in a schoolgirlish way. 'Oh, this is M. Poirot, an old friend of mine. We met by chance just outside here. Actually I hit him with an apple core. Like William Tell — only the other way about.'

'How d'you do, M. Poirot. Robin.'

'Yes, Madre?'

'Get some drinks. Where are the cigarettes?'

'On that table.'

Mrs Upward asked: 'Are you a writer, too, M. Poirot?'

'Oh, no,' said Mrs Oliver. 'He's a detective. You know. The Sherlock Holmes kind — deerstalkers and violins and all that. And he's come here to solve a murder.'

There was a faint tinkle of broken glass. Mrs Upward said sharply: 'Robin, do be careful.' To Poirot she said: 'That's very interesting, M. Poirot.'

'So Maureen Summerhayes was right,' exclaimed Robin. 'She told me some long rigmarole about having a detective on the premises. She seemed to think it was frightfully funny. But it's really quite serious, isn't it?'

'Of course it's serious,' said Mrs Oliver. 'You've got a criminal in your midst.'

'Yes, but look here, who's been murdered? Or is it someone that's been dug up and it's all frightfully hush hush?'

'It is not hush hush,' said Poirot. 'The murder, you know about it already.'

'Mrs Mc — something — a charwoman — last autumn,' said Mrs Oliver.

'Oh!' Robin Upward sounded disappointed. 'But that's all over.'

'It's not over at all,' said Mrs Oliver. 'They arrested the wrong man, and he'll be hanged if M. Poirot doesn't find the real murderer in time. It's all frightfully exciting.'

Robin apportioned the drinks.

'White Lady for you, Madre.'

'Thank you, my dear boy.'

Poirot frowned slightly. Robin handed drinks to Mrs Oliver and to him.

'Well,' said Robin, 'here's to crime.'

He drank.

'She used to work here,' he said.

'Mrs McGinty?' asked Mrs Oliver.

'Yes. Didn't she, Madre?'

'When you say work here, she came one day a week.'

'And odd afternoons sometimes.'

'What was she like?' asked Mrs Oliver.

'Terribly respectable,' said Robin. 'And maddeningly tidy. She had a ghastly way of tidying up everything and putting things into drawers so that you simply couldn't guess where they were.'

Mrs Upward said with a certain grim humour:

'If somebody didn't tidy things away at least one day a week, you soon wouldn't be able to move in this small house.'

'I know, Madre, I know. But unless things are left where I put them, I simply can't work at all. My notes get all disarranged.'

'It's annoying to be as helpless as I am,' said Mrs Upward. 'We have a faithful old maid, but it's all she can manage just to do a little simple cooking.'

'What is it?' asked Mrs Oliver. 'Arthritis?'

'Some form of it. I shall have to have a permanent nurse-companion soon, I'm afraid. Such a bore. I like being independent.'

'Now, darling,' said Robin. 'Don't work yourself up.'

He patted her arm.

She smiled at him with sudden tenderness.

'Robin's as good as a daughter to me,' she said. 'He does everything — and thinks of everything. No one could be more considerate.'

They smiled at each other.

Hercule Poirot rose.

'Alas,' he said. 'I must go. I have another call to make and then a train to catch. Madame, I thank you for your hospitality. Mr Upward, I wish all success to the play.'

'And all success to you with your murder,' said Mrs Oliver.

'Is this really serious, M. Poirot?' asked Robin Upward. 'Or is it a terrific hoax?'

'Of course it isn't a hoax,' said Mrs Oliver. 'It's deadly serious. He won't tell me who the murderer is, but he knows, don't you?'

'No, no, madame,' Poirot's protest was just sufficiently unconvincing. 'I told you that as yet, no, I do not know.'

'That's what you said, but I think you do know really . . . But you're so frightfully secretive, aren't you?'

Mrs Upward said sharply:

'Is this really true? It's not a joke?'

'It is not a joke, madame,' said Poirot.

He bowed and departed.

As he went down the path he heard Robin Upward's clear tenor voice:

'But Ariadne, darling,' he said, 'it's all very well, but with that moustache and everything, how *can* one take him seriously? Do you really mean he's *good*?'

Poirot smiled to himself. Good indeed!

About to cross the narrow lane, he jumped back just in time.

The Summerhayes' station wagon, lurching and bumping, came racing past him. Summerhayes was driving.

'Sorry,' he called. 'Got to catch train.' And faintly from the distance: 'Covent Garden . . .'

Poirot also intended to take a train — the local train to Kilchester, where he had arranged a conference with Superintendent Spence.

He had time, before catching it, for just one last call.

He went to the top of the hill and through gates and up a well-kept drive to a modern house of frosted concrete with a square roof and a good deal of window. This was the home of Mr and Mrs Carpenter. Guy

Carpenter was a partner in the big Carpenter Engineering Works — a very rich man who had recently taken to politics. He and his wife had only been married a short time.

The Carpenters' front door was not opened by foreign help, or an aged faithful. An imperturbable manservant opened the door and was loath to admit Hercule Poirot. In his view Hercule Poirot was the kind of caller who is left outside. He clearly suspected that Hercule Poirot had come to sell something.

'Mr and Mrs Carpenter are not at home.'

'Perhaps, then, I might wait?'

'I couldn't say when they will be in.'

He closed the door.

Poirot did not go down the drive. Instead he walked round the corner of the house and almost collided with a tall young woman in a mink coat.

'Hallo,' she said. 'What the hell do you want?'

Poirot raised his hat with gallantry.

'I was hoping,' he said, 'that I could see Mr or Mrs Carpenter. Have I the pleasure of seeing Mrs Carpenter?'

'I'm Mrs Carpenter.'

She spoke ungraciously, but there was a faint suggestion of appeasement behind her manner.

'My name is Hercule Poirot.'

Nothing registered. Not only was the great, the unique name unknown to her, but he thought that she did not even identify him as Maureen Summerhayes' latest guest. Here, then, the local grape vine did not operate. A small but significant fact, perhaps.

'Yes?'

'I demand to see either Mr or Mrs Carpenter, but you, madame, will be the best for my purpose. For what I have to ask is of domestic matters.'

'We've got a Hoover,' said Mrs Carpenter suspiciously.

Poirot laughed.

'No, no, you misunderstand. It is only a few questions that I ask about a domestic matter.'

'Oh, you mean one of these domestic questionnaires. I do think it's absolutely idiotic — ' She broke off. 'Perhaps you'd better come inside.'

Poirot smiled faintly. She had just stopped herself from uttering a derogatory comment. With her husband's political activities, caution in criticizing Government activities was indicated.

She led the way through the hall and into a good-sized room giving on to a carefully tended garden. It was a very new-looking room, a large brocaded suite of sofa and two wing-chairs, three or four reproductions of Chippendale chairs, a bureau, a writing desk. No expense had been spared, the best firms had been employed, and there was absolutely no sign of individual taste. The bride, Poirot thought, had been what? Indifferent? Careful?

He looked at her appraisingly as she turned. An expensive and good-looking young woman. Platinum blonde hair, carefully applied make-up, but something more — wide cornflower blue eyes — eyes with a wide frozen stare in them — beautiful drowned eyes.

She said — graciously now, but concealing boredom:

'Do sit down.'

He sat. He said:

'You are most amiable, madame. These questions now that I wish to ask you. They relate to a Mrs McGinty who died — was killed that is to say — last November.'

'Mrs McGinty? I don't know what you mean?'

She was glaring at him. Her eyes hard and suspicious.

'You remember Mrs McGinty?'

'No, I don't. I don't know anything about her.'

'You remember her murder? Or is murder

132

so common here that you do not even notice it?'

'Oh, the *murder*? Yes, of course. I'd forgotten what the old woman's name was.'

'Although she worked for you in this house?'

'She didn't. I wasn't living here then. Mr Carpenter and I were only married three months ago.'

'But she did work for you. On Friday mornings, I think it was. You were then Mrs Selkirk and you lived in Rose Cottage.'

She said sulkily:

'If you know the answers to everything I don't see why you need to ask questions. Anyway, what's it all about?'

'I am making an investigation into the circumstances of the murder.'

'Why? What on earth for? Anyway, why come to me?'

'You might know something — that would help me.'

'I don't know anything at all. Why should I? She was only a stupid old charwoman. She kept her money under the floor and somebody robbed and murdered her for it. It was quite disgusting — beastly, the whole thing. Like things you read in the Sunday papers.'

Poirot took that up quickly.

'Like the Sunday papers, yes. Like the *Sunday Comet*. You read, perhaps, the *Sunday Comet*?'

She jumped up, and made her way, blunderingly, towards the opened French windows. So uncertainly did she go that she actually collided with the window frame. Poirot was reminded of a beautiful big moth, fluttering blindly against a lamp shade.

She called: 'Guy — Guy!'

A man's voice a little way away answered: 'Eve?'

'Come here quickly.'

A tall man of about thirty-five came into sight. He quickened his pace and came across the terrace to the window. Eve Carpenter said vehemently:

'There's a man here — a foreigner. He's asking me all sorts of questions about that horrid murder last year. Some old char-woman — you remember? I *hate* things like that. You know I do.'

Guy Carpenter frowned and came into the drawing-room through the window. He had a long face like a horse, he was pale and looked rather supercilious. His manner was pompous.

Hercule Poirot found him unattractive.

'May I ask what all this is about?' he asked. 'Have you been annoying my wife?'

Hercule Poirot spread out his hands.

'The last thing I should wish is to annoy so charming a lady. I hoped only that, the deceased woman having worked for her, she might be able to aid me in the investigations I am making.'

'But — what are these investigations?'

'Yes, ask him that,' urged his wife.

'A fresh inquiry is being made into the circumstances of Mrs McGinty's death.'

'Nonsense — the case is over.'

'No, no, there you are in error. It is not over.'

'A fresh inquiry, you say?' Guy Carpenter frowned. He said suspiciously: 'By the police? Nonsense — you're nothing to do with the police.'

'That is correct. I am working independently of the police.'

'It's the Press,' Eve Carpenter broke in. 'Some horrid Sunday newspaper. He said so.'

A gleam of caution came into Guy Carpenter's eye. In his position he was not anxious to antagonize the Press. He said, more amicably:

'My wife is very sensitive. Murders and things like that upset her. I'm sure it can't be necessary for you to bother her. She hardly knew this woman.'

Eve said vehemently:

'She was only a stupid old charwoman. I told him so.'

She added:

'And she was a frightful liar, too.'

'Ah, that is interesting.' Poirot turned a beaming face from one to the other of them. 'So she told lies. That may give us a very valuable lead.'

'I don't see how,' said Eve sulkily.

'The establishment of motive,' said Poirot. 'That is the line I am following up.'

'She was robbed of her savings,' said Carpenter sharply. 'That was the motive of the crime.'

'Ah,' said Poirot softly. 'But was it?'

He rose like an actor who had just spoken a telling line.

'I regret if I have caused madame any pain,' he said politely. 'These affairs are always rather unpleasant.'

'The whole business was distressing,' said Carpenter quickly. 'Naturally my wife didn't like being reminded of it. I'm sorry we can't help you with any information.'

'Oh, but you have.'

'I beg your pardon?'

Poirot said softly:

'*Mrs McGinty told lies*. A valuable fact. What lies, exactly, did she tell, madame?'

He waited politely for Eve Carpenter to

speak. She said at last:

'Oh, nothing particular. I mean — I can't remember.'

Conscious perhaps, that both men were looking at her expectantly, she said:

'Stupid things — about people. Things that couldn't be true.'

Still there was a silence, then Poirot said:

'I see — she had a dangerous tongue.'

Eve Carpenter made a quick movement.

'Oh no — I didn't mean as much as that. She was just a gossip, that was all.'

'Just a gossip,' said Poirot softly.

He made a gesture of farewell.

Guy Carpenter accompanied him out into the hall.

'This paper of yours — this Sunday paper — which is it?'

'The paper I mentioned to madame,' replied Poirot carefully, 'was the *Sunday Comet*.'

He paused. Guy Carpenter repeated thoughtfully:

'The *Sunday Comet*. I don't very often see that, I'm afraid.'

'It has interesting articles sometimes. And interesting illustrations . . . '

Before the pause could be too long, he bowed, and said quickly:

'Au revoir, Mr Carpenter. I am sorry if I

have — disturbed you.'

Outside the gate, he looked back at the house.

'I wonder,' he said. 'Yes, I wonder . . . '

11

Superintendent Spence sat opposite Hercule Poirot and sighed.

'I'm not saying you haven't got anything, M. Poirot,' he said slowly. 'Personally, I think you have. But it's thin. It's terribly thin!'

Poirot nodded.

'By itself it will not do. There must be more.'

'My sergeant or I ought to have spotted that newspaper.'

'No, no, you cannot blame yourself. The crime was so obvious. Robbery with violence. The room all pulled about, the money missing. Why should there be significance to you in a torn newspaper amongst the other confusion.'

Spence repeated obstinately:

'I should have got that. And the bottle of ink — '

'I heard of that by the merest chance.'

'Yet it meant something to you — why?'

'Only because of that chance phrase about writing a letter. You and I, Spence, we write so many letters — to us it is such a matter of course.'

Superintendent Spence sighed. Then he laid out on the table four photographs.

'These are the photos you asked me to get — the original photos that the *Sunday Comet* used. At any rate they're a little clearer than the reproductions. But upon my word, they're not much to go upon. Old, faded — and with women the hair-do makes a difference. There's nothing definite in any of them to go upon like ears or a profile. That *cloche* hat and that arty hair and the roses! Doesn't give you a chance.'

'You agree with me that we can discard Vera Blake?'

'I should think so. If Vera Blake was in Broadhinny, everyone would know it — telling the sad story of her life seems to have been her speciality.'

'What can you tell me about the others?'

'I've got what I could for you in the time. Eva Kane left the country after Craig was sentenced. And I can tell you the name she took. It was Hope. Symbolic, perhaps?'

Poirot murmured:

'Yes, yes — the romantic approach. *'Beautiful Evelyn Hope is dead.'* A line from one of your poets. I dare say she thought of that. Was her name Evelyn, by the way?'

'Yes, I believe it was. But Eva was what she was known as always. And by the way, M.

Poirot, now that we're on the subject, the police opinion of Eva Kane doesn't quite square with this article here. Very far from it.'

Poirot smiled.

'What the police think — it is not evidence. But it is usually a very sound guide. What did the police think of Eva Kane?'

'That she was by no means the innocent victim that the public thought her. I was quite a young chap at the time and remember hearing it discussed by my old Chief and Inspector Traill who was in charge of the case. Traill believed (no evidence, mind you) that the pretty little idea of putting Mrs Craig out of the way was all Eva Kane's idea — and that she not only thought of it, but she did it. Craig came home one day and found his little friend had taken a short cut. She thought it would all pass off as natural death, I dare say. But Craig knew better. He got the wind up and disposed of the body in the cellar and elaborated the plan of having Mrs Craig die abroad. Then, when the whole thing came out, he was frantic in his assertions that he'd done it alone, that Eva Kane had known nothing about it. Well,' Superintendent Spence shrugged his shoulders, 'nobody could prove anything else. The stuff was in the house. Either of them could have used it. Pretty Eva Kane was all innocence and horror. Very well she did it, too: a clever little actress. Inspector Traill had his doubts — but there was nothing to go upon. I'm giving you that for what it's worth, M. Poirot. It's not evidence.'

'But it suggests the possibility that one, at least, of these 'tragic women' was something more than a tragic woman — that she was a murderess and that, if the incentive was strong enough, she might murder again . . . And now the next one, Janice Courtland, what can you tell me about her?'

'I've looked up the files. A nasty bit of goods. If we hanged Edith Thompson we certainly ought to have hanged Janice Courtland. An unpleasant pair, she and her husband, nothing to choose between them, and she worked on that young man until she had him all up in arms. But all the time, mark you, there was a rich man in the background, and it was to marry him she wanted her husband out of the way.'

'Did she marry him?'

Spence shook his head.

'No idea.'

'She went abroad — and then?'

Spence shook his head.

'She was a free woman. She'd not been charged with anything. Whether she married, or what happened to her, we don't know.'

'One might meet her at a cocktail party any day,' said Poirot, thinking of Dr Rendell's remark.

'Exactly.'

Poirot shifted his gaze to the last photograph.

'And the child? Lily Gamboll?'

'Too young to be charged with murder. She was sent to an approved school. Good record there. Was taught shorthand and typing and was found a job under probation. Did well. Last heard of in Ireland. I think we could wash her out, you know, M. Poirot, same as Vera Blake. After all, she'd made good, and people don't hold it against a kid of twelve for doing something in a fit of temper. What about washing her out?'

'I might,' said Poirot, 'if it were not for the chopper. It is undeniable that Lily Gamboll used a chopper on her aunt, and the unknown killer of Mrs McGinty used something that was said to be like a chopper.'

'Perhaps you're right. Now, M. Poirot, let's have your side of things. Nobody's tried to do you in, I'm glad to see.'

'N-no,' said Poirot, with a momentary hesitation.

'I don't mind telling you I've had the wind up about you once or twice since that evening in London. Now what are the possibilities amongst the residents of Broadhinny?'

Poirot opened his little notebook.

'Eva Kane, if she is still alive, would be now approaching sixty. Her daughter, of whose adult life our *Sunday Comet* paints such a touching picture, would be now in the thirties. Lily Gamboll would also be about that age. Janice Courtland would now be not far short of fifty.'

Spence nodded agreement.

'So we come to the residents of Broadhinny, with especial reference to those for whom Mrs McGinty worked.'

'That last is a fair assumption, I think.'

'Yes, it is complicated by the fact that Mrs McGinty did occasional odd work here and there, but we will assume for the time being that she saw whatever she did see, presumably a photograph, at one of her regular 'houses'.'

'Agreed.'

'Then as far as age goes, that gives us as possibles — first the Wetherbys where Mrs McGinty worked on the day of her death. Mrs Wetherby is the right age for Eva Kane and she has a daughter of the right age to be Eva Kane's daughter — a daughter said to be by a previous marriage.'

'And as regards the photograph?'

'*Mon cher*, no positive identification from

that is possible. Too much time has passed, too much water, as you say, has flowed from the waterworks. One can but say this: Mrs Wetherby has been, decidedly, a pretty woman. She has all the mannerisms of one. She seems much too fragile and helpless to do murder, but then that was, I understand, the popular belief about Eva Kane. How much actual physical strength would have been needed to kill Mrs McGinty is difficult to say without knowing exactly what weapon was used, its handle, the ease with which it could be swung, the sharpness of its cutting edge, etcetera.'

'Yes, yes. Why we never managed to find that — but go on.'

'The only other remarks I have to make about the Wetherby household are that Mr Wetherby could make himself, and I fancy does make himself, very unpleasant if he likes. The daughter is fanatically devoted to her mother. She hates her stepfather. I do not remark on these facts. I present them, only for consideration. Daughter might kill to prevent mother's past coming to stepfather's ears. Mother might kill for same reason. Father might kill to prevent 'scandal' coming out. More murders have been committed for respectability than one would believe possible! The Wetherbys are 'nice people'.'

Spence nodded.

'If — I say if — there is anything in this *Sunday Comet* business, then the Wetherbys are clearly the best bet,' he said.

'Exactly. The only other person in Broadhinny who would fit in age with Eva Kane is Mrs Upward. There are two arguments against Mrs Upward, as Eva Kane, having killed Mrs McGinty. First, she suffers from arthritis, and spends most of her time in a wheeled chair — '

'In a book,' said Spence enviously, 'that wheeled chair business would be phoney, but in real life it's probably all according to Cocker.'

'Secondly,' continued Poirot, 'Mrs Upward seems of a dogmatic and forceful disposition, more inclined to bully than to coax, which does not agree with the accounts of our young Eva. On the other hand, people's characters do develop and self-assertiveness is a quality that often comes with age.'

'That's true enough,' conceded Spence. 'Mrs Upward — not impossible but unlikely. Now the other possibilities. Janice Courtland?'

'Can, I think, be ruled out. There is no one in Broadhinny the right age.'

'Unless one of the younger women is Janice Courtland with her face lifted. Don't mind me — just my little joke.'

'There are three women of thirty-odd. There is Deirdre Henderson. There is Dr Rendell's wife, and there is Mrs Guy Carpenter. That is to say, any one of these *could* be Lily Gamboll or alternatively Eva Kane's daughter as far as age goes.'

'And as far as possibility goes?'

Poirot sighed.

'Eva Kane's daughter may be tall or short, dark or fair — we have no guide to what she looks like. We have considered Deirdre Henderson in that role. Now for the other two. First of all I will tell you this: Mrs Rendell is afraid of something.'

'Afraid of you?'

'I think so.'

'That might be significant,' said Spence slowly. 'You're suggesting that Mrs Rendell might be Eva Kane's daughter *or* Lily Gamboll. Is she fair or dark?'

'Fair.'

'Lily Gamboll was a fair-haired child.'

'Mrs Carpenter is also fair-haired. A most expensively made-up young woman. Whether she is actually good-looking or not, she has very remarkable eyes. Lovely wide-open dark-blue eyes.'

'Now, Poirot — ' Spence shook his head at his friend.

'Do you know what she looked like as she ran out of the room to call her husband? I was reminded of a lovely fluttering moth. She blundered into the furniture and stretched her hands out like a blind thing.'

Spence looked at him indulgently.

'Romantic, that's what you are, M. Poirot,' he said. 'You and your lovely fluttering moths and wide-open blue eyes.'

'Not at all,' said Poirot. 'My friend Hastings, *he* was romantic and sentimental, me never! Me, I am severely practical. What I am telling you is that if a girl's claims to beauty depend principally on the loveliness of her eyes, then, no matter how short-sighted she is, she will take off her spectacles and learn to feel her way round even if outlines are blurred and distance hard to judge.'

And gently, with his forefinger, he tapped the photograph of the child Lily Gamboll in the thick disfiguring spectacles.

'So that's what you think? Lily Gamboll?'

'No, I speak only of what might be. At the time Mrs McGinty died Mrs Carpenter was not yet Mrs Carpenter. She was a young war widow, very badly off, living in a labourer's cottage. She was engaged to be married to the rich man of the neighbourhood — a man with political ambitions and a great sense of his own importance. If Guy Carpenter had

148

found out that he was about to marry, say, a child of low origin who had obtained notoriety by hitting her aunt on the head with a chopper, or alternatively the daughter of Craig, one of the most notorious criminals of the century — prominently placed in your Chamber of Horrors — well, one asks would he have gone through with it? You say perhaps, if he loved the girl, yes! But he is not quite that kind of man. I would put him down as selfish, ambitious, and a man very nice in the manner of his reputation. I think that if young Mrs Selkirk, as she was then, was anxious to achieve the match she would have been very very anxious that no hint of an unfortunate nature got to her fiancé's ears.'

'I see, you think it's her, do you?'

'I tell you again, *mon cher, I do not know.* I examine only possibilities. Mrs Carpenter was on her guard against me, watchful, alarmed.'

'That looks bad.'

'Yes, yes, but it is all very difficult. Once I stayed with some friends in the country and they went out to do the shooting. You know the way it goes? One walks with the dogs and the guns, and the dogs, they put up the game — it flies out of the woods, up into the air and you go bang bang. That is like us. It is not only one bird we put up, perhaps, there are other birds in the covert. Birds, perhaps, with which we have nothing to do. But the birds themselves do not know that. We must make very sure, *cher ami*, which is *our* bird. During Mrs Carpenter's widowhood, there may have been indiscretions — no worse than that, but still inconvenient. Certainly there must be some reason why she says to me quickly that Mrs McGinty was a liar!'

Superintendent Spence rubbed his nose.

'Let's get this clear, Poirot. What *do* you really think?'

'What I think does not matter. I must *know*. And as yet, the dogs have only just gone into the covert.'

Spence murmured: 'If we could get anything at all definite. One really suspicious circumstance. As it is, it's all theory and rather far-fetched theory at that. The whole thing's thin, you know, as I said. *Does* anyone really murder for the reasons we've been considering?'

'That depends,' said Poirot. 'It depends on a lot of family circumstances we do not know. But the passion for respectability is very strong. These are not artists or Bohemians. Very nice people live in Broadhinny. My postmistress said so. And nice people like to preserve their niceness. Years of happy married life, maybe, no suspicion that you were once a notorious figure in one of the most sensational murder trials, no suspicion that your child is the child of a famous murderer. One might say 'I would rather die than have my husband know!' Or 'I would rather die than have my daughter discover who she is!' And then you would go on to reflect that it would be better, perhaps, if Mrs McGinty died . . . '

Spence said quietly:

'So you think it's the Wetherbys.'

'No. They fit the best, perhaps, but that is all. In actual character, Mrs Upward is a more *likely* killer than Mrs Wetherby. She has determination and willpower and she fairly dotes on her son. To prevent his learning of what happened before she married his father and settled down to respectable married bliss, I think she might go far.'

'Would it upset him so much?'

'Personally I do not think so. Young Robin has a modern sceptical point of view, is thoroughly selfish, and in any case is less devoted, I should say, to his mother than she to him. He is not another James Bentley.'

'Granting Mrs Upward *was* Eva Kane, her son Robin wouldn't kill Mrs McGinty to prevent the fact coming out?'

'Not for a moment, I should say. He would

probably capitalize on it. Use the fact for publicity for his plays! I can't see Robin Upward committing a murder for respectability, or devotion, or in fact for anything but a good solid gain to Robin Upward.'

Spence sighed. He said: 'It's a wide field. We may be able to get something on the past history of these people. But it will take time. The war has complicated things. Records destroyed — endless opportunities for people who want to cover their traces doing so by means of other people's identity cards, etc., especially after 'incidents' when nobody could know which corpse was which! If we could concentrate on just *one* lot, but you've got so many possibles, M. Poirot.'

'We may be able to cut them down soon.'

Poirot left the superintendent's office with less cheerfulness in his heart than he had shown in his manner. He was obsessed as Spence was, by the urge of time. If only he could have *time* . . .

And farther back still was the one teasing doubt — was the edifice he and Spence had built up really sound? Supposing, after all, that James Bentley *was* guilty . . .

He did not give in to that doubt, but it worried him.

Again and again he had gone over in his mind the interview he had had with James

Bentley. He thought of it now whilst he waited on the platform at Kilchester for his train to come in. It had been market day and the platform was crowded. More crowds were coming in through the barriers.

Poirot leaned forward to look. Yes, the train was coming at last. Before he could right himself he felt a sudden hard purposeful shove in the small of his back. It was so violent and so unexpected that he was taken completely unawares. In another second he would have fallen on the line under the incoming train, but a man beside him on the platform caught hold of him in the nick of time, pulling him back.

'Why, whatever came over you?' he demanded. He was a big burly Army sergeant. 'Taken queer? Man, you were nearly under the train.'

'I thank you. I thank you a thousand times.' Already the crowd was milling round them, boarding the train, others leaving it.

'All right now? I'll help you in.'

Shaken, Poirot subsided on to a seat.

Useless to say 'I was pushed,' but he *had* been pushed. Up till that very evening he had gone about consciously on his guard, on the alert for danger. But after talking with Spence, after Spence's bantering inquiry as to whether any attempt on his life had been

153

made, he had insensibly regarded the danger as over or unlikely to materialize.

But how wrong he had been! Amongst those he had interviewed in Broadhinny one interview had achieved a result. Somebody had been afraid. Somebody had sought to put an end to his dangerous resuscitation of a closed case.

From a call-box in the station at Broadhinny, Poirot rang up Superintendent Spence.

'It is you, *mon ami*? Attend, I pray. I have news for you. Splendid news. *Somebody has tried to kill me . . .* '

He listened with satisfaction to the flow of remarks from the other end.

'No, I am not hurt. But it was a very near thing . . . Yes, under a train. No, I did not see who did it. But be assured, my friend, *I shall find out.* We know now — that we are on the right track.'

12

The man who was testing the electric meter passed the time of day with Guy Carpenter's superior manservant, who was watching him.

'Electricity's going to operate on a new basis,' he explained. 'Graded flat rate according to occupancy.'

The superior butler remarked sceptically:

'What you mean is it's going to cost more like everything else.'

'That depends. Fair shares for all, that's what I say. Did you go in to the meeting at Kilchester last night?'

'No.'

'Your boss, Mr Carpenter, spoke very well, they say. Think he'll get in?'

'It was a near shave last time, I believe.'

'Yes. A hundred and twenty-five majority, something like that. Do you drive him in to these meetings, or does he drive himself?'

'Usually drives himself. Likes driving. He's got a Rolls Bentley.'

'Does himself well. Mrs Carpenter drive too?'

'Yes. Drives a lot too fast, in my opinion.'

'Women usually do. Was she at the meeting last night too? Or isn't she interested in politics?'

The superior butler grinned.

'Pretends she is, anyway. However, she didn't stick it out last night. Had a headache or something and left in the middle of the speeches.'

'Ah!' The electrician peered into the fuse boxes. 'Nearly done now,' he remarked. He put a few more desultory questions as he collected his tools and prepared to depart.

He walked briskly down the drive, but round the corner from the gateway he stopped and made an entry in his pocket book.

'*C. Drove home alone last night.
Reached home 10.30 (approx.). Could
have been at Kilchester Central Station
time indicated. Mrs C. left meeting
early. Got home only ten minutes
before C. Said to have come home by
train.*'

It was the second entry in the electrician's book. The first ran:

'Dr R. *Called out on case last night. Direction of Kilchester. Could have been at Kilchester Central Station at time indicated. Mrs R. alone all evening in house(?) After taking coffee in, Mrs Scott, housekeeper, did not see her again that night. Has small car of her own.*'

II

At Laburnums, collaboration was in process.

Robin Upward was saying earnestly:

'You do see, don't you, what a wonderful line that is? And if we really get a feeling of sex antagonism between the chap and the girl it'll pep the whole thing up enormously!'

Sadly, Mrs Oliver ran her hands through her windswept grey hair, causing it to look as though swept not by wind but by a tornado.

'You do see what I mean, don't you, Ariadne darling?'

'Oh, I see what you *mean*,' said Mrs Oliver gloomily.

'But the main thing is for you to feel really happy about it.'

Nobody but a really determined self-deceiver could have thought that Mrs Oliver looked happy.

Robin continued blithely:

'What I feel is, here's that wonderful young man, parachuted down — '

Mrs Oliver interrupted:

'He's sixty.'

'Oh *no*!'

'He is.'

'I don't *see* him like that. Thirty-five — not a day older.'

'But I've been writing books about him for thirty years, and he was at least thirty-five in the first one.'

'But, darling, if he's sixty, you can't have the tension between him and the girl — what's her name? Ingrid. I mean, it would make him just a nasty old man!'

'It certainly would.'

'So you see, he *must* be thirty-five,' said Robin triumphantly.

'Then he can't be Sven Hjerson. Just make him a Norwegian young man who's in the Resistance Movement.'

'But darling Ariadne, the whole *point* of the play is Sven Hjerson. You've got an enormous public who simply *adore* Sven Hjerson, and who'll flock to see Sven Hjerson. He's *box office*, darling!'

'But people who read my books *know* what he's like! You can't invent an entirely new young man in the Norwegian Resistance

Movement and just *call* him Sven Hjerson.'

'Ariadne darling, I *did* explain all that. It's not a *book*, darling, it's a *play*. And we've just got to have glamour! And if we get this tension, this antagonism between Sven Hjerson and this — what's-her-name? — Karen — you know, all against each other and yet really frightfully attracted — '

'Sven Hjerson never cared for women,' said Mrs Oliver coldly.

'But you *can't* have him a *pansy*, darling. Not for *this* sort of play. I mean it's not green bay trees or anything like *that*. It's thrills and murders and clean open-air fun.'

The mention of open air had its effect.

'I think I'm going out,' said Mrs Oliver abruptly. 'I need air. I need air *badly*.'

'Shall I come with you?' asked Robin tenderly.

'No, I'd rather go alone.'

'Just as you like, darling. Perhaps you're right. I'd better go and whip up an egg nog for Madre. The poor sweet is feeling just a teeny weeny bit left out of things. She *does* like attention, you know. And you'll think about that scene in the cellar, won't you? The whole thing is coming really wonderfully well. It's going to be the most tremendous success. I *know* it is!'

Mrs Oliver sighed.

'But the main thing,' continued Robin, 'is for you to feel happy about it!'

Casting a cold look at him, Mrs Oliver threw a showy military cape which she had once bought in Italy about her ample shoulders and went out into Broadhinny.

She would forget her troubles, she decided, by turning her mind to the elucidation of real crime. Hercule Poirot needed help. She would take a look at the inhabitants of Broadhinny, exercise her woman's intuition which had never failed, and tell Poirot who the murderer was. Then he would only have to get the necessary evidence.

Mrs Oliver started her quest by going down the hill to the post office and buying two pounds of apples. During the purchase, she entered into amicable conversation with Mrs Sweetiman.

Having agreed that the weather was very warm for the time of year, Mrs Oliver remarked that she was staying with Mrs Upward at Laburnums.

'Yes, I know. You'll be the lady from London that writes the murder books? Three of them I've got here now in Penguins.'

Mrs Oliver cast a glance over the Penguin display. It was slightly overlaid by children's waders.

'*The Affair of the Second Goldfish,*' she

mused, 'that's quite a good one. *The Cat it was Who Died* — that's where I made a blowpipe a foot long and it's really six feet. Ridiculous that a blowpipe should be that size, but someone wrote from a museum to tell me so. Sometimes I think there are people who only read books in the hope of finding mistakes in them. What's the other one of them? Oh! *Death of a Débutante* — that's frightful tripe! I made sulphonal soluble in water and it isn't, and the whole thing is wildly impossible from start to finish. At least eight people die before Sven Hjerson gets his brainwave.'

'Very popular they are,' said Mrs Sweetiman, unmoved by this interesting self-criticism. 'You wouldn't believe! I've never read any myself, because I don't really get time for reading.'

'You had a murder of your own down here, didn't you?' said Mrs Oliver.

'Yes, last November that was. Almost next door here, as you might say.'

'I hear there's a detective down here, looking into it?'

'Ah, you mean the little foreign gentleman up at Long Meadows? He was in here only yesterday and — '

Mrs Sweetiman broke off as another customer entered for stamps.

She bustled round to the post office side.

'Good morning, Miss Henderson. Warm for the time of year today.'

'Yes, it is.'

Mrs Oliver stared hard at the tall girl's back. She had a Sealyham with her on a lead.

'Means the fruit blossom will get nipped later!' said Mrs Sweetiman, with gloomy relish. 'How's Mrs Wetherby keeping?'

'Fairly well, thank you. She hasn't been out much. There's been such an east wind lately.'

'There's a very good picture on at Kilchester this week, Miss Henderson. You ought to go.'

'I thought of going last night, but I couldn't really bother.'

'It's Betty Grable next week — I'm out of 5s. books of stamps. Will two 2s. 6d. ones do you?'

As the girl went out, Mrs Oliver said:

'Mrs Wetherby's an invalid, isn't she?'

'That's as may be,' Mrs Sweetiman replied rather acidly. 'There's some of us as hasn't the time to lay by.'

'I do so agree with you,' said Mrs Oliver. 'I tell Mrs Upward that if she'd only make more of an effort to use her legs it would be better for her.'

Mrs Sweetiman looked amused.

'She gets about when she wants to — or so I've heard.'

'Does she now?'

Mrs Oliver considered the source of information.

'Janet?' she hazarded.

'Janet Groom grumbles a bit,' said Mrs Sweetiman. 'And you can hardly wonder, can you? Miss Groom's not so young herself and she has the rheumatism cruel bad when the wind's in the east. But archititis, it's called, when it's the gentry has it, *and* invalid chairs and what not. Ah well, I wouldn't risk losing the use of my legs, I wouldn't. But there, nowadays even if you've got a chilblain you run to the doctor with it so as to get your money's worth out of the National Health. Too much of this health business we've got. Never did you any good thinking how bad you feel.'

'I expect you're right,' said Mrs Oliver.

She picked up her apples and went out in pursuit of Deirdre Henderson. This was not difficult, since the Sealyham was old and fat and was enjoying a leisurely examination of tufts of grass and pleasant smells.

Dogs, Mrs Oliver considered, were always a means of introduction.

'What a darling!' she exclaimed.

The big young woman with the plain face looked gratified.

'He *is* rather attractive,' she said. 'Aren't you, Ben?'

Ben looked up, gave a slight wiggle of his sausage-like body, resumed his nasal inspection of a tuft of thistles, approved it and proceeded to register approval in the usual manner.

'Does he fight?' asked Mrs Oliver. 'Sealyhams do very often.'

'Yes, he's an awful fighter. That's why I keep him on the lead.'

'I thought so.'

Both women considered the Sealyham.

Then Deirdre Henderson said with a kind of rush:

'You're — you're Ariadne Oliver, aren't you?'

'Yes. I'm staying with the Upwards.'

'I know. Robin told us you were coming. I must tell you how much I enjoy your books.'

Mrs Oliver, as usual, went purple with embarrassment.

'Oh,' she murmured unhappily. 'I'm very glad,' she added gloomily.

'I haven't read as many of them as I'd like to, because we get books sent down from the Times Book Club and Mother doesn't like detective stories. She's frightfully sensitive and they keep her awake at night. But I adore them.'

'You've had a real crime down here, haven't you?' said Mrs Oliver. 'Which house was it? One of these cottages?'

'That one there.'

Deirdre Henderson spoke in a rather choked voice.

Mrs Oliver directed her gaze on Mrs McGinty's former dwelling, the front door-step of which was at present occupied by two unpleasant little Kiddles who were happily torturing a cat. As Mrs Oliver stepped forward to remonstrate, the cat escaped by a firm use of its claws.

The eldest Kiddle, who had been severely scratched, set up a howl.

'Serves you right,' said Mrs Oliver, adding to Deirdre Henderson: 'It doesn't *look* like a house where there's been a murder, does it?'

'No, it doesn't.'

Both women seemed to be in accord about that.

Mrs Oliver continued:

'An old charwoman, wasn't it, and somebody robbed her?'

'Her lodger. She had some money — under the floor.'

'I see.'

Deirdre Henderson said suddenly:

'But perhaps it wasn't him after all. There's a funny little man down here — a foreigner. His name's Hercule Poirot — '

'Hercule Poirot? Oh yes, I know all about him.'

'Is he really a detective?'

'My dear, he's frightfully celebrated. And terribly clever.'

'Then perhaps he'll find out that he didn't do it after all.'

'Who?'

'The — the lodger. James Bentley. Oh, I do hope he'll get off.'

'Do you? Why?'

'Because I don't want it to be him. I never wanted it to be him.'

Mrs Oliver looked at her curiously, startled by the passion in her voice.

'Did you know him?'

'No,' said Deirdre slowly, 'I didn't *know* him. But once Ben got his foot caught in a trap and he helped me to get him free. And we talked a little . . . '

'What was he like?'

'He was dreadfully lonely. His mother had just died. He was frightfully fond of his mother.'

'And you are very fond of yours?' said Mrs Oliver acutely.

'Yes. That made me understand. Understand what he felt, I mean. Mother and I — we've just got each other, you see.'

'I thought Robin told me that you had a stepfather.'

Deirdre said bitterly: 'Oh yes, I've got a *step*father.'

Mrs Oliver said vaguely: 'It's not the same thing, is it, as one's own father. Do you remember your own father?'

'No, he died before I was born. Mother married Mr Wetherby when I was four years old. I — I've always hated him. And Mother — ' She paused before saying: 'Mother's had a very sad life. She's had no sympathy or understanding. My stepfather is a most unfeeling man, hard and cold.'

Mrs Oliver nodded, and then murmured:

'This James Bentley doesn't sound at all like a criminal.'

'I never thought the police would arrest *him*. I'm sure it must have been some tramp. There are horrid tramps along this road sometimes. It must have been one of them.'

Mrs Oliver said consolingly:

'Perhaps Hercule Poirot will find out the truth.'

'Yes, perhaps — '

She turned off abruptly into the gateway of Hunter's Close.

Mrs Oliver looked after her for a moment or two, then drew a small notebook from her handbag. In it she wrote: 'Not Deirdre Henderson,' and underlined the *not* so firmly that the pencil broke.

III

Half-way up the hill she met Robin Upward coming down it with a handsome platinum-haired young woman.

Robin introduced them.

'This is the wonderful Ariadne Oliver, Eve,' he said. 'My dear, I don't know *how* she does it. Looks so benevolent, too, doesn't she? Not at all as though she wallowed in crime. This is Eve Carpenter. Her husband is going to be our next Member. The present one, Sir George Cartwright, is quite gaga, poor old man. He jumps out at young girls from behind doors.'

'Robin, you mustn't invent such terrible lies. You'll discredit the Party.'

'Well, why should *I* care? It isn't my Party. I'm a Liberal. That's the only Party it's possible to belong to nowadays, really small and select, and without a chance of getting in. I adore lost causes.'

He added to Mrs Oliver:

'Eve wants us to come in for drinks this evening. A sort of party for you, Ariadne. You know, meet the lion. We're all terribly terribly thrilled to have you here. Can't you put the scene of your next murder in Broadhinny?'

'Oh do, Mrs Oliver,' said Eve Carpenter.

'You can easily get Sven Hjerson down here,' said Robin. 'He can be like Hercule Poirot, staying at the Summerhayes' Guest House. We're just going there now because I told Eve, Hercule Poirot is just as much a celebrity in his line as you are in yours, and she says she was rather rude to him yesterday, so she's going to ask him to the party too. But seriously, dear, do make your next murder happen in Broadhinny. We'd all be so thrilled.'

'Oh do, Mrs Oliver. It would be such fun,' said Eve Carpenter.

'Who shall we have as murderer and who as victim,' asked Robin.

'Who's your present charwoman?' asked Mrs Oliver.

'Oh my dear, not *that* kind of murder. So dull. No, I think Eve here would make rather a nice victim. Strangled, perhaps, with her own nylon stockings. No, that's been done.'

'I think *you'd* better be murdered, Robin,' said Eve. 'The coming playwright, stabbed in country cottage.'

'We haven't settled on a murderer yet,' said Robin. 'What about my Mamma? Using her wheeled chair so that there wouldn't be footprints. I think that would be lovely.'

'She wouldn't want to stab you, though, Robin.'

Robin considered.

'No, perhaps not. As a matter of fact I was considering her strangling *you*. She wouldn't mind doing that half as much.'

'But I want *you* to be the victim. And the person who kills you can be Deirdre Henderson. The repressed plain girl whom nobody notices.'

'There you are, Ariadne,' said Robin. 'The whole plot of your next novel presented to you. All you'll have to do is work in a few false clues, and — of course — do the actual writing. Oh, goodness, what terrible dogs Maureen does have.'

They had turned in at the gate of Long Meadows, and two Irish wolfhounds had rushed forward, barking.

Maureen Summerhayes came out into the stableyard with a bucket in her hand.

'Down, Flyn. Come here, Cormic. Hallo. I'm just cleaning out Piggy's stable.'

'We know that, darling,' said Robin. 'We can smell you from here. How's Piggy getting along?'

'We had a terrible fright about him yesterday. He was lying down and he didn't want his breakfast. Johnnie and I read up all the diseases in the Pig Book and couldn't sleep for worrying about him, but this morning he was frightfully well and gay and absolutely charged Johnnie when Johnnie came in with his food. Knocked him flat, as a matter of fact. Johnnie had to go and have a bath.'

'What exciting lives you and Johnnie lead,' said Robin.

Eve said: 'Will you and Johnnie come in and have drinks with us this evening, Maureen?'

'Love to.'

'To meet Mrs Oliver,' said Robin, 'but actually you can meet her now. This is she.'

'Are you really?' said Maureen. 'How thrilling. You and Robin are doing a play together, aren't you?'

'It's coming along splendidly,' said Robin. 'By the way, Ariadne, I had a brainwave after you went out this morning. About casting.'

'Oh, casting,' said Mrs Oliver in a relieved voice.

'I know just the right person to play Eric. Cecil Leech — he's playing in the Little Rep at Cullenquay. We'll run over and see the show one evening.'

'We want your P.G.,' said Eve to Maureen. 'Is he about? I want to ask him tonight, too.'

'We'll bring him along,' said Maureen.

'I think I'd better ask him myself. As a matter of fact I was a bit rude to him yesterday.'

'Oh! Well, he's somewhere about,' said Maureen vaguely. 'In the garden, I think — Cormic — Flyn — those damned dogs — ' She dropped the bucket with a clatter and ran in the direction of the duck pond, whence a furious quacking had arisen.

13

Mrs Oliver, glass in hand, approached Hercule Poirot towards the end of the Carpenters' party. Up till that moment they had each of them been the centre of an admiring circle. Now that a good deal of gin had been consumed, and the party was going well, there was a tendency for old friends to get together and retail local scandal, and the two outsiders were able to talk to each other.

'Come out on the terrace,' said Mrs Oliver, in a conspirator's whisper.

At the same time she pressed into his hand a small piece of paper.

Together they stepped out through the French windows and walked along the terrace. Poirot unfolded the piece of paper.

'Dr Rendell,' he read.

He looked questioningly at Mrs Oliver. Mrs Oliver nodded vigorously, a large plume of grey hair falling across her face as she did so.

'He's the murderer,' said Mrs Oliver.

'You think so? Why?'

'I just know it,' said Mrs Oliver. 'He's the *type*. Hearty and genial, and all that.'

'Perhaps.'

Poirot sounded unconvinced.

'But what would you say was his motive?'

'Unprofessional conduct,' said Mrs Oliver. 'And Mrs McGinty knew about it. But whatever the reason was, you can be quite sure it was him. I've looked at all the others, and he's the one.'

In reply, Poirot remarked conversationally:

'Last night somebody tried to push me on to the railway line at Kilchester station.'

'Good gracious. To kill you, do you mean?'

'I have no doubt that was the idea.'

'And Dr Rendell was out on a case, I know he was.'

'I understand — yes — that Dr Rendell *was* out on a case.'

'Then that settles it,' said Mrs Oliver with satisfaction.

'Not quite,' said Poirot. 'Both Mr and Mrs Carpenter were in Kilchester last night and came home separately. Mrs Rendell may have sat at home all the evening listening to her wireless or she may not — no one can say. Miss Henderson often goes to the pictures in Kilchester.'

'She didn't last night. She was at home. She told me so.'

'You cannot believe all you are told,' said Poirot reprovingly. 'Families hang together.

The foreign maid, Frieda, on the other hand, *was* at the pictures last night, so she cannot tell us who was or was not at home at Hunter's Close! You see, it is not so easy to narrow things down.'

'I can probably vouch for our lot,' said Mrs Oliver. 'What time did you say this happened?'

'At nine thirty-five exactly.'

'Then at any rate Laburnums has got a clean bill of health. From eight o'clock to half-past ten, Robin, his mother, and I were playing poker patience.'

'I thought possibly that you and he were closeted together doing the collaboration?'

'Leaving Mamma to leap on a motor bicycle concealed in the shrubbery?' Mrs Oliver laughed. 'No, Mamma was under our eye.' She sighed as sadder thoughts came to her. 'Collaboration,' she said bitterly. 'The whole thing's a nightmare! How would *you* like to see a big black moustache stuck on to Superintendent Battle and be told it was *you*.'

Poirot blinked a little.

'But it is a nightmare, that suggestion!'

'Now you know what I suffer.'

'I, too, suffer,' said Poirot. 'The cooking of Madame Summerhayes, it is beyond description. It is not cooking at all. And the

175

draughts, the cold winds, the upset stomachs of the cats, the long hairs of the dogs, the broken legs of the chairs, the terrible, terrible bed in which I sleep' — he shut his eyes in remembrance of agonies — 'the tepid water in the bathroom, the holes in the stair carpet, and the coffee — words cannot describe to you the fluid which they serve to you as coffee. It is an affront to the stomach.'

'Dear me,' said Mrs Oliver. 'And yet, you know, she's awfully nice.'

'Mrs Summerhayes? She is charming. She is quite charming. That makes it much more difficult.'

'Here she comes now,' said Mrs Oliver.

Maureen Summerhayes was approaching them.

There was an ecstatic look on her freckled face. She carried a glass in her hand. She smiled at them both with affection.

'I think I'm a bit tiddly,' she announced. 'Such lots of lovely gin. I do like parties! We don't often have one in Broadhinny. It's because of you both being so celebrated. I wish *I* could write books. The trouble with me is, I can't do *anything* properly.'

'You are a good wife and mother, madame,' said Poirot primly.

Maureen's eyes opened. Attractive hazel eyes in a small freckled face. Mrs Oliver wondered how old she was. Not much more than thirty, she guessed.

'Am I?' said Maureen. 'I wonder. I love them all terribly, but is that enough?'

Poirot coughed.

'If you will not think me presumptuous, madame. A wife who truly loves her husband should take great care of his stomach. It is important, the stomach.'

Maureen looked slightly affronted.

'Johnnie's got a wonderful stomach,' she said indignantly. 'Absolutely flat. Practically not a stomach at all.'

'I was referring to what is put inside it.'

'You mean my cooking,' said Maureen. 'I never think it matters much *what* one eats.'

Poirot groaned.

'Or what one wears,' said Maureen dreamily. 'Or what one does. I don't think *things* matter — not really.'

She was silent for a moment or two, her eyes alcoholically hazy, as though she was looking into the far distance.

'There was a woman writing in the paper the other day,' she said suddenly. 'A really stupid letter. Asking what was best to do — to let your child be adopted by someone who could give it every advantage — *every advantage*, that's what she said — and she meant a good education, and clothes and comfortable surroundings — or whether to keep it when you couldn't give it advantages of any kind. I think that's stupid — *really* stupid. If you can just give a child enough to eat — that's all that matters.'

She stared down into her empty glass as though it were a crystal.

'*I* ought to know,' she said. 'I was an adopted child. My mother parted with me and I had every advantage, as they call it. And it's always hurt — always — always — to know that you weren't really wanted, that your mother could let you go.'

'It was a sacrifice for your good, perhaps,' said Poirot.

Her clear eyes met his.

'I don't think that's ever true. It's the way they put it to themselves. But what it boils down to is that they can, really, get on without you . . . And it hurts. I wouldn't give up *my* children — not for all the advantages in the world!'

'I think you're quite right,' said Mrs Oliver.

'And I, too, agree,' said Poirot.

'Then that's all right,' said Maureen cheerfully. 'What are we arguing about?'

Robin, who had come along the terrace to join them, said:

'Yes, what are you arguing about?'

'Adoption,' said Maureen. 'I don't like

being adopted, do you?'

'Well, it's much better than being an orphan, don't you think so, darling? I think we ought to go now, don't you, Ariadne?'

The guests left in a body. Dr Rendell had already had to hurry away. They walked down the hill together talking gaily with that extra hilarity that a series of cocktails induces.

When they reached the gate of Laburnums, Robin insisted that they should all come in.

'Just to tell Madre all about the party. So boring for her, poor sweet, not to have been able to go because her leg was playing her up. But she so hates being left out of things.'

They surged in cheerfully and Mrs Upward seemed pleased to see them.

'Who else was there?' she asked. 'The Wetherbys?'

'No, Mrs Wetherby didn't feel well enough, and that dim Henderson girl wouldn't come without her.'

'She's really rather pathetic, isn't she?' said Shelagh Rendell.

'I think almost pathological, don't you?' said Robin.

'It's that mother of hers,' said Maureen. 'Some mothers really do almost eat their young, don't they?'

She flushed suddenly as she met Mrs Upward's quizzical eye.

'Do I devour you, Robin?' Mrs Upward asked.

'Madre! Of course not!'

To cover her confusion Maureen hastily plunged into an account of her breeding experiences with Irish wolfhounds. The conversation became technical.

Mrs Upward said decisively:

'You can't get away from heredity — in people as well as dogs.'

Shelagh Rendell murmured:

'Don't you think it's environment?'

Mrs Upward cut her short.

'No, my dear, I don't. Environment can give a veneer — no more. It's what's bred in people that counts.'

Hercule Poirot's eyes rested curiously on Shelagh Rendell's flushed face. She said with what seemed unnecessary passion:

'But that's cruel — unfair.'

Mrs Upward said: 'Life is unfair.'

The slow lazy voice of Johnnie Summerhayes joined in.

'I agree with Mrs Upward. Breeding tells. That's been my creed always.'

Mrs Oliver said questioningly: 'You mean things are handed down. Unto the third or fourth generation — '

Maureen Summerhayes said suddenly in her sweet high voice:

'But that quotation goes on: 'And show mercy unto thousands.' '

Once again everybody seemed a little embarrassed, perhaps at the serious note that had crept into the conversation.

They made a diversion by attacking Poirot.

'Tell us all about Mrs McGinty, M. Poirot. Why didn't the dreary lodger kill her?'

'He used to mutter, you know,' said Robin. 'Walking about in the lanes. I've often met him. And really, definitely, he looked frightfully queer.'

'You must have some reason for thinking he didn't kill her, M. Poirot. Do tell us.'

Poirot smiled at them. He twirled his moustache.

'If he didn't kill her, who did?'

'Yes, who did?'

Mrs Upward said drily: 'Don't embarrass the man. He probably suspects one of us.'

'One of us? Oo!'

In the clamour Poirot's eyes met those of Mrs Upward. They were amused and — something else — challenging?

'He suspects one of us,' said Robin delightedly. 'Now then, Maureen,' he assumed the manner of a bullying K.C., 'Where were you on the night of the — what night *was* it?'

'November 22nd,' said Poirot.

'On the night of the 22nd?'

'Gracious, I don't know,' said Maureen.

'Nobody could know after all this time,' said Mrs Rendell.

'Well, I can,' said Robin. 'Because I was broadcasting that night. I drove to Coalport to give a talk on Some Aspects of the Theatre. I remember because I discussed Galsworthy's charwoman in the Silver Box at great length and the next day Mrs McGinty was killed and I wondered if the charwoman in the play had been like her.'

'That's right,' said Shelagh Rendell suddenly. 'And I remember now because you said your mother would be all alone because it was Janet's night off, and I came down here after dinner to keep her company. Only unfortunately I couldn't make her hear.'

'Let me think,' said Mrs Upward. 'Oh! Yes, of course. I'd gone to bed with a headache and my bedroom faces the back garden.'

'And next day,' said Shelagh, 'when I heard Mrs McGinty had been killed, I thought, 'Oo! I might have passed the murderer in the dark' — because at first we all thought it must have been some tramp who broke in.'

'Well, I still don't remember what I was doing,' said Maureen. 'But I do remember the next morning. It was the baker told us. 'Old Mrs McGinty's been done in,' he said.

And there I was, wondering why she hadn't turned up as usual.'

She gave a shiver.

'It's horrible really, isn't it?' she said.

Mrs Upward was still watching Poirot.

He thought to himself: 'She is a very intelligent woman — and a ruthless one. Also selfish. In whatever she did, she would have no qualms and no remorse . . .'

A thin voice was speaking — urging, querulous.

'Haven't you got *any* clues, M. Poirot?'

It was Shelagh Rendell.

Johnnie Summerhayes' long dark face lit up enthusiastically.

'That's it, clues,' he said. 'That's what I like in detective stories. Clues that mean everything to the detective — and nothing to you — until the end when you fairly kick yourself. Can't you give us one little clue, M. Poirot?'

Laughing, pleading faces turned to him. A game to them all (or perhaps not to one of them?). But murder wasn't a game — murder was dangerous. You never knew.

With a sudden brusque movement, Poirot pulled out four photographs from his pocket.

'You want a clue?' he said. '*Voilà!*'

And with a dramatic gesture he tossed them down on the table.

They clustered round, bending over, and uttering ejaculations.

'*Look!*'

'What frightful frumps!'

'Just look at the roses. '*Rowses, rowses, all the way!*' '

'My dear, that *hat!*'

'What a frightful child!'

'But who are they?'

'Aren't fashions ridiculous?'

'That woman must really have been rather good-looking once.'

'But why are they clues?'

'Who are they?'

Poirot looked slowly round at the circle of faces.

He saw nothing other than he might have expected to see.

'You do not recognize any of them?'

'Recognize?'

'You do not, shall I say, remember having seen any of those photographs before? But yes — Mrs Upward? You recognize something, do you not?'

Mrs Upward hesitated.

'Yes — I think — '

'Which one?'

Her forefinger went out and rested on the spectacled child-like face of Lily Gamboll.

'You have seen that photograph — when?'

'Quite recently . . . Now where — no, I can't remember. But I'm sure I've seen a photograph just like that.'

She sat frowning, her brows drawn together.

She came out of her abstraction as Mrs Rendell came to her.

'Goodbye, Mrs Upward. I do hope you'll come to tea with me one day if you feel up to it.'

'Thank you, my dear. If Robin pushes me up the hill.'

'Of course, Madre. I've developed the most tremendous muscles pushing that chair. Do you remember the day we went to the Wetherbys and it was so muddy — '

'Ah!' said Mrs Upward suddenly.

'What is it, Madre?'

'Nothing. Go on.'

'Getting you up the hill again. First the chair skidded and then I skidded. I thought we'd never get home.'

Laughing, they took their leave and trooped out.

Alcohol, Poirot thought, certainly loosens the tongue.

Had he been wise or foolish to display those photographs? Had that gesture also been the result of alcohol?

He wasn't sure.

But, murmuring an excuse, he turned back.

He pushed open the gate and walked up to the house. Through the open window on his left he heard the murmur of two voices. They were the voices of Robin and Mrs Oliver. Very little of Mrs Oliver and a good deal of Robin.

Poirot pushed the door open and went through the right-hand door into the room he had left a few moments before. Mrs Upward was sitting before the fire. There was a rather grim look on her face. She had been so deeply in thought that his entry startled her.

At the sound of the apologetic little cough he gave, she looked up sharply, with a start.

'Oh,' she said. 'It's you. You startled me.'

'I am sorry, madame. Did you think it was someone else? Who did you think it was?'

She did not answer that, merely said:

'Did you leave something behind?'

'What I feared I had left was danger.'

'Danger?'

'Danger, perhaps, to you. Because you recognized one of those photographs just now.'

'I wouldn't say recognized. All old photographs look exactly alike.'

'Listen, madame. Mrs McGinty also, or so I believe, recognized one of those photographs. *And Mrs McGinty is dead.*'

With an unexpected glint of humour in her eye, Mrs Upward said:

'*Mrs McGinty's dead. How did she die? Sticking her neck out just like I.* Is that what you mean?'

'Yes. If you know anything — anything at all, tell it to me now. It will be safer so.'

'My dear man, it's not nearly so simple as that. I'm not at all sure that I do know anything — certainly nothing as definite as a *fact*. Vague recollections are very tricky things. One would have to have some idea of how and where and when, if you follow what I mean.'

'But it seems to me that you already have that idea.'

'There is more to it than that. There are various factors to be taken into consideration. Now it's no good your rushing me, M. Poirot. I'm not the kind of person who rushes into decisions. I've a mind of my own, and I take time to make it up. When I come to a decision, I act. But not till I'm ready.'

'You are in many ways a secretive woman, madame.'

'Perhaps — up to a point. Knowledge is power. Power must only be used for the right ends. You will excuse my saying that you don't perhaps appreciate the pattern of our English country life.'

'In other words you say to me, 'You are only a damned foreigner.' '

Mrs Upward smiled slightly.

'I shouldn't be as rude as that.'

'If you do not want to talk to me, there is Superintendent Spence.'

'My dear M. Poirot. Not the police. Not at this stage.'

He shrugged his shoulders.

'I have warned you,' he said.

For he was sure that by now Mrs Upward remembered quite well exactly when and where she had seen the photograph of Lily Gamboll.

14

I

'Decidedly,' said Hercule Poirot to himself the following morning, 'the spring is here.'

His apprehensions of the night before seemed singularly groundless.

Mrs Upward was a sensible woman who could take good care of herself.

Nevertheless in some curious way, she intrigued him. He did not at all understand her reactions. Clearly she did not want him to. She had recognized the photograph of Lily Gamboll and she was determined to play a lone hand.

Poirot, pacing a garden path while he pursued these reflections, was startled by a voice behind him.

'M. Poirot.'

Mrs Rendell had come up so quietly that he had not heard her. Since yesterday he had felt extremely nervous.

'Pardon, madame. You made me jump.'

Mrs Rendell smiled mechanically. If he were nervous, Mrs Rendell, he thought, was

189

even more so. There was a twitching in one of her eyelids and her hands worked restlessly together.

'I — I hope I'm not interrupting you. Perhaps you're busy.'

'But no, I am not busy. The day is fine. I enjoy the feeling of spring. It is good to be outdoors. In the house of Mrs Summerhayes there is always, but always, the current of air.'

'The current — '

'What in England you call a draught.'

'Yes. Yes, I suppose there is.'

'The windows, they will not shut and the doors they fly open all the time.'

'It's rather a ramshackle house. And of course, the Summerhayes are so badly off they can't afford to do much to it. I'd let it go if I were them. I know it's been in their family for hundreds of years, but nowadays you just can't cling on to things for sentiment's sake.'

'No, we are not sentimental nowadays.'

There was a silence. Out of the corner of his eye, Poirot watched those nervous white hands. He waited for her to take the initiative. When she did speak it was abruptly.

'I suppose,' she said, 'that when you are, well, investigating a thing, you'd always have to have a pretext?'

Poirot considered the question. Though he did not look at her, he was perfectly aware of her eager sideways glance fixed on him.

'As you say, madame,' he replied non-committally. 'It is a convenience.'

'To explain your being there, and — and asking things.'

'It might be expedient.'

'Why — why are you really here in Broadhinny, M. Poirot?'

He turned a mild surprised gaze on her.

'But, my dear lady, I told you — to inquire into the death of Mrs McGinty.'

Mrs Rendell said sharply:

'I know that's what you say. But it's ridiculous.'

Poirot raised his eyebrows.

'Is it?'

'Of course it is. Nobody believes it.'

'And yet I assure you, it is a simple fact.'

Her pale blue eyes blinked and she looked away.

'You won't tell me.'

'Tell you — what, madame?'

She changed the subject abruptly again, it seemed.

'I wanted to ask you — about anonymous letters.'

'Yes,' said Poirot encouragingly as she stopped.

'They're really always lies, aren't they?'

'They are sometimes lies,' said Poirot cautiously.

'Usually,' she persisted.

'I don't know that I would go as far as saying that.'

Shelagh Rendell said vehemently:

'They're cowardly, treacherous, *mean* things!'

'All that, yes, I would agree.'

'And you wouldn't ever believe what was said in one, would you?'

'That is a very difficult question,' said Poirot gravely.

'I wouldn't. I wouldn't believe anything of that kind.'

She added vehemently:

'I know why you're down here. And it isn't true, I tell you, it isn't true.'

She turned sharply and walked away.

Hercule Poirot raised his eyebrows in an interested fashion.

'And now what?' he demanded of himself. 'Am I being taken up the garden walk? Or is this the bird of a different colour?'

It was all, he felt, very confusing.

Mrs Rendell professed to believe that he was down here for a reason other than that of inquiring into Mrs McGinty's death. She had suggested that that was only a pretext.

Did she really believe that? Or was she, as he had just said to himself, leading him up the garden walk?

What had anonymous letters got to do with it?

Was Mrs Rendell the original of the photograph that Mrs Upward had said she had 'seen recently'?

In other words, was Mrs Rendell Lily Gamboll? Lily Gamboll, a rehabilitated member of society, had been last heard of in Eire. Had Dr Rendell met and married his wife there, in ignorance of her history? Lily Gamboll had been trained as a stenographer. Her path and the doctor's might easily have crossed.

Poirot shook his head and sighed.

It was all perfectly possible. But he had to be sure.

A chilly wind sprang up suddenly and the sun went in.

Poirot shivered and retraced his steps to the house.

Yes, he had to be sure. If he could find the actual weapon of the murder —

And at that moment, with a strange feeling of certainty — he *saw it*.

II

Afterwards he wondered whether, subconsciously, he had seen and noted it much earlier. It had stood there, presumably, ever since he had come to Long Meadows . . .

There on the littered top of the bookcase near the window.

He thought: 'Why did I never notice that before?'

He picked it up, weighed it in his hands, examined it, balanced it, raised it to strike —

Maureen came in through the door with her usual rush, two dogs accompanying her. Her voice, light and friendly, said:

'Hallo, are you playing with the sugar cutter?'

'Is that what it is? A sugar cutter?'

'Yes. A sugar cutter — or a sugar hammer — I don't know what exactly is the right term. It's rather fun, isn't it? So childish with the little bird on top.'

Poirot turned the implement carefully in his hands. Made of much ornamented brass, it was shaped like an adze, heavy, with a sharp cutting edge. It was studded here and there with coloured stones, pale blue and red. On top of it was a frivolous little bird with turquoise eyes.

'Lovely thing for killing anyone, wouldn't it

194

be?' said Maureen conversationally.

She took it from him and aimed a murderous blow at a point in space.

'Frightfully easy,' she said. 'What's that bit in the Idylls of the King? ' '*Mark's way,' he said, and clove him to the brain.'* I should think you could cleave anyone to the brain with this all right, don't you?'

Poirot looked at her. Her freckled face was serene and cheerful.

She said:

'I've told Johnnie what's coming to him if I get fed up with him. I call it the wife's best friend!'

She laughed, put the sugar hammer down and turned towards the door.

'What did I come in here for?' she mused. 'I can't remember . . . Bother! I'd better go and see if that pudding needs more water in the saucepan.'

Poirot's voice stopped her before she got to the door.

'You brought this back with you from India, perhaps?'

'Oh no,' said Maureen. 'I got it at the B. and B. at Christmas.'

'B. and B.?' Poirot was puzzled.

'Bring and Buy,' explained Maureen glibly. 'At the Vicarage. You bring things you don't want, and you buy something. Something not too frightful if you can find it. Of course there's practically never anything you really want. I got this and that coffee pot. I like the coffee pot's nose and I liked the little bird on the hammer.'

The coffee pot was a small one of beaten copper. It had a big curving spout that struck a familiar note to Poirot.

'I think they come from Baghdad,' said Maureen. 'At least I think that's what the Wetherbys said. Or it may have been Persia.'

'It was from the Wetherbys' house, then, that these came?'

'Yes. They've got a most frightful lot of junk. I *must* go. That pudding.'

She went out. The door banged. Poirot picked up the sugar cutter again and took it to the window.

On the cutting edge were faint, very faint, discolorations.

Poirot nodded his head.

He hesitated for a moment, then he carried the sugar hammer out of the room and up to his bedroom. There he packed it carefully in a box, did the whole thing up neatly in paper and string, and going downstairs again, left the house.

He did not think that anyone would notice the disappearance of the sugar cutter. It was not a tidy household.

III

At Laburnums, collaboration was pursuing its difficult course.

'But I really don't feel it's right making him a vegetarian, darling,' Robin was objecting. 'Too faddy. And definitely not glamorous.'

'I can't help it,' said Mrs Oliver obstinately. 'He's *always* been a vegetarian. He takes round a little machine for grating raw carrots and turnips.'

'But, Ariadne, precious, *why?*'

'How do I know?' said Mrs Oliver crossly. 'How do I know why I ever thought of the revolting man? I must have been mad! Why a Finn when I know nothing about Finland? Why a vegetarian? Why all the idiotic manerisms he's got? These things just *happen*. You try something — and people seem to like it — and then you go on — and before you know where you are, you've got someone like that maddening Sven Hjerson tied to you for life. And people even write and say how fond you must be of him. Fond of him? If I met that bony, gangling, vegetable-eating Finn in real life, I'd do a better murder than any I've ever invented.'

Robin Upward gazed at her with reverence.

'You know, Ariadne, that might be rather a marvellous idea. A real Sven Hjerson — and

197

you murder him. You might make a Swan Song book of it — to be published after your death.'

'No fear!' said Mrs Oliver. 'What about the money? Any money to be made out of murders I want now.'

'Yes. Yes. There I couldn't agree with you more.'

The harassed playwright strode up and down.

'This Ingrid creature is getting rather tiresome,' he said. 'And after the cellar scene which is really going to be marvellous, I don't quite see how we're going to prevent the next scene from being rather an anti-climax.'

Mrs Oliver was silent. Scenes, she felt, were Robin Upward's headache.

Robin shot a dissatisfied glance at her.

That morning, in one of her frequent changes of mood, Mrs Oliver had disliked her windswept coiffure. With a brush dipped in water she had plastered her grey locks close to her skull. With her high forehead, her massive glasses, and her stern air, she was reminding Robin more and more of a school teacher who had awed his early youth. He found it more and more difficult to address her as darling, and even flinched at 'Ariadne'.

He said fretfully:

'You know, I don't feel a bit in the mood

today. All that gin yesterday, perhaps. Let's scrap work and go into the question of casting. If we can get Denis Callory, of course it will be too marvellous, but he's tied up in films at the moment. And Jean Bellews for Ingrid would be just right — and she *wants* to play it which is so nice. Eric — as I say, I've had a brainwave for Eric. We'll go over to the Little Rep tonight, shall we? And you'll tell me what you think of Cecil for the part.'

Mrs Oliver agreed hopefully to this project and Robin went off to telephone.

'There,' he said returning. 'That's all fixed.'

IV

The fine morning had not lived up to its promise. Clouds had gathered and the day was oppressive with a threat of rain. As Poirot walked through the dense shrubberies to the front door of Hunter's Close, he decided that he would not like to live in this hollow valley at the foot of the hill. The house itself was closed in by trees and its walls suffocated in ivy. It needed, he thought, the woodman's axe.

(The axe? The sugar cutter?)

He rang the bell and after getting no response, rang it again.

It was Deirdre Henderson who opened the door to him. She seemed surprised.

'Oh,' she said, 'it's you.'

'May I come in and speak to you?'

'I — well, yes, I suppose so.'

She led him into the small dark sitting-room where he had waited before. On the mantelpiece he recognized the big brother of the small coffee pot on Maureen's shelf. Its vast hooked nose seemed to dominate the small Western room with a hint of Eastern ferocity.

'I'm afraid,' said Deirdre in an apologetic tone, 'that we're rather upset today. Our help, the German girl — she's going. She's only been here a month. Actually it seems she just took this post to get over to this country because there was someone she wanted to marry. And now they've fixed it up, and she's going straight off tonight.'

Poirot clicked his tongue.

'Most inconsiderate.'

'It is, isn't it? My stepfather says it isn't legal. But even if it isn't legal, if she just goes off and gets married, I don't see what one can do about it. We shouldn't even have known she *was* going if I hadn't found her packing her clothes. She would just have walked out of the house without a word.'

'It is, alas, not an age of consideration.'

'No,' said Deirdre dully. 'I suppose it's not.'

She rubbed her forehead with the back of her hand.

'I'm tired,' she said. 'I'm very tired.'

'Yes,' said Poirot gently. 'I think you may be very tired.'

'What was it you wanted, M. Poirot?'

'I wanted to ask you about a sugar hammer.'

'A sugar hammer?'

Her face was blank, uncomprehending.

'An instrument of brass, with a bird on it, and inlaid with blue and red and green stones.' Poirot enunciated the description carefully.

'Oh yes, I know.'

Her voice showed no interest or animation.

'I understand it came from this house?'

'Yes. My mother bought it in the bazaar at Baghdad. It's one of the things we took to the Vicarage sale.'

'The Bring and Buy sale, that is right?'

'Yes. We have a lot of them here. It's difficult to get people to give money, but there's usually something you can rake up and send.'

'So it was here, in this house, until Christmas, and then you sent it to the Bring and Buy sale? Is that right?'

Deirdre frowned.

'Not the Christmas Bring and Buy. It was the one before. The Harvest Festival one.'

'The Harvest Festival — that would be — when? October? September?'

'The end of September.'

It was very quiet in the little room. Poirot looked at the girl and she looked back at him. Her face was mild, expressionless, uninterested. Behind the blank wall of her apathy, he tried to guess what was going on. Nothing, perhaps. Perhaps she was, as she had said, just tired . . .

He said, quietly, urgently:

'You are quite sure it was the Harvest Festival Sale? Not the Christmas one?'

'Quite sure.'

Her eyes were steady, unblinking.

Hercule Poirot waited. He continued to wait . . .

But what he was waiting for did not come.

He said formally:

'I must not keep you any longer, mademoiselle.'

She went with him to the front door.

Presently he was walking down the drive again.

Two divergent statements — statements that could not possibly be reconciled.

Who was right? Maureen Summerhayes or Deirdre Henderson?

If the sugar cutter had been used as he believed it had been used, the point was vital. The Harvest Festival had been the end of September. Between then and Christmas, on November 22nd, Mrs McGinty had been killed. Whose property had the sugar cutter been at the time?

He went to the post office. Mrs Sweetiman was always helpful and she did her best. She'd been to both sales, she said. She always went. You picked up many a nice bit there. She helped, too, to arrange things beforehand. Though most people brought things with them and didn't send them beforehand.

A brass hammer, rather like an axe, with coloured stones and a little bird? No, she couldn't rightly remember. There was such a lot of things, and so much confusion and some things snatched up at once. Well, perhaps she did remember something like that — priced at five shillings it had been, and with a copper coffee pot, but the pot had got a hole in the bottom — you couldn't use it, only for ornament. But she couldn't remember when it was — some time ago. Might have been Christmas, might have been before. She hadn't been noticing . . .

She accepted Poirot's parcel. Registered? Yes.

She copied down the address; he noticed

just a sharp flicker of interest in her keen black eyes as she handed him the receipt.

Hercule Poirot walked slowly up the hill, wondering to himself.

Of the two, Maureen Summerhayes, scatter-brained, cheerful, inaccurate, was the more likely to be wrong. Harvest or Christmas, it would be all one to her.

Deirdre Henderson, slow, awkward, was far more likely to be accurate in her identification of times and dates.

Yet there remained that irking question.

Why, after his questions, hadn't she asked him *why he wanted to know?* Surely a natural, an almost inevitable, question?

But Deirdre Henderson hadn't asked it.

15

I

'Someone rang you up,' called Maureen from the kitchen as Poirot entered the house.

'Rang me up? Who was that?'

He was slightly surprised.

'Don't know, but I jotted the number down on my ration book.'

'Thank you, Madame.'

He went into the dining-room and over to the desk. Amongst the litter of papers he found the ration book lying near the telephone and the words — Kilchester 350.

Raising the receiver of the telephone, he dialled the number.

Immediately a woman's voice said:

'Breather and Scuttle.'

Poirot made a quick guess.

'Can I speak to Miss Maude Williams?'

There was a moment's interval and then a contralto voice said:

'Miss Williams speaking.'

'This is Hercule Poirot. I think you rang me.'

'Yes — yes, I did. It's about the property you were asking me about the other day.'

'The property?' For a moment Poirot was puzzled. Then he realized that Maude's conversation was being overheard. Probably she had telephoned him before when she was alone in the office.

'I understand you, I think. It is the affair of James Bentley and Mrs McGinty's murder.'

'That's right. Can we do anything in the matter for you?'

'You want to help. You are not private where you are?'

'That's right.'

'I understand. Listen carefully. You really want to help James Bentley?'

'Yes.'

'Would you resign your present post?'

There was no hesitation.

'Yes.'

'Would you be willing to take a domestic post? Possibly with not very congenial people?'

'Yes.'

'Could you get away at once? By tomorrow, for instance?'

'Oh yes, M. Poirot. I think that could be managed.'

'You understand what I want you to do. You would be a domestic help — to live in. You can cook?'

A faint amusement tinged the voice.

'Very well.'

'*Bon Dieu,* what a rarity! Now listen, I am coming into Kilchester at once. I will meet you in the same café where I met you before, at lunch time.'

'Yes, certainly.'

Poirot rang off.

'An admirable young woman,' he reflected. 'Quick-witted, knows her own mind — perhaps, even, she can cook . . . '

With some difficulty he disinterred the local telephone directory from under a treatise on pigkeeping and looked up the Wetherbys' number.

The voice that answered him was that of Mrs Wetherby.

''Allo?' Allo? It is M. Poirot — you remember, Madame — '

'I don't think I — '

'M. Hercule Poirot.'

'Oh yes — of course — do forgive me. Rather a domestic upset today — '

'It is for that reason exactly I rang you up. I am desolated to learn of your difficulties.'

'So ungrateful — these foreign girls. Her fare paid over here, and everything. I do so hate ingratitude.'

'Yes, yes. I do indeed sympathize. It is monstrous — that is why I hasten to tell you that I have, perhaps, a solution. By the merest chance I know of a young woman wanting a domestic post. Not, I fear, fully trained.'

'Oh, there's no such thing as training nowadays. Will she cook — so many of them won't cook.'

'Yes — yes — she cooks. Shall I then send her to you — at least on trial? Her name is Maude Williams.'

'Oh, please do, M. Poirot. It's most kind of you. Anything would be better than nothing. My husband is so particular and gets so annoyed with dear Deirdre when the household doesn't go smoothly. One can't expect men to understand how difficult everything is nowadays — I — '

There was an interruption. Mrs Wetherby spoke to someone entering the room, and though she had placed her hand over the receiver Poirot could hear her slightly muffled words.

'It's that little detective man — knows of someone to come in to replace Frieda. No, not foreign — English, thank goodness. Very kind of him, really, he seems quite concerned about me. Oh, darling, don't make objections. What does it *matter?* You know the absurd way Roger goes on. Well, I think it's very kind — and I don't suppose she's too awful.'

The asides over, Mrs Wetherby spoke with the utmost graciousness.

'Thank you very much, M. Poirot. We are most grateful.'

Poirot replaced the receiver and glanced at his watch.

He went to the kitchen.

'Madame, I shall not be in to lunch. I have to go to Kilchester.'

'Thank goodness,' said Maureen. 'I didn't get to that pudding in time. It had boiled dry. I think it's really all right — just a little scorched perhaps. In case it tasted rather nasty I thought I would open a bottle of those raspberries I put up last summer. They seem to have a bit of mould on top but they say nowadays that that doesn't matter. It's really rather good for you — practically penicillin.'

Poirot left the house, glad that scorched pudding and near-penicillin were not to be his portion today. Better — far better — eat macaroni and custard and plums at the Blue Cat than the improvisations of Maureen Summerhayes.

II

At Laburnums a little friction had arisen.

'Of course, Robin, you never seem to remember anything when you are working on a play.'

Robin was contrite.

'Madre, I am most terribly sorry. I'd forgotten all about it's being Janet's night out.'

'It doesn't matter at all,' said Mrs Upward coldly.

'Of course it matters. I'll ring up the Rep and tell them we'll go tomorrow night instead.'

'You'll do nothing of the sort. You've arranged to go tonight and you'll go.'

'But really — '

'That's settled.'

'Shall I ask Janet to go out another night?'

'Certainly *not*. She hates to have her plans disarranged.'

'I'm sure she wouldn't really mind. Not if I put it to her — '

'You'll do nothing of the sort, Robin. Please don't go upsetting Janet. And don't go on about it. I don't care to feel I'm a tiresome old woman spoiling other people's pleasure.'

'Madre — sweetest — '

'That's enough — you go and enjoy

yourselves. I know who I'll ask to keep me company.'

'Who?'

'That's my secret,' said Mrs Upward, her good humour restored. 'Now stop fussing, Robin.'

'I'll ring up Shelagh Rendell — '

'I'll do my own ringing up, thank you. It's all settled. Make the coffee before you go, and leave it by me in the percolator ready to switch on. Oh, and you might as well put out an extra cup — in case I have a visitor.'

16

Sitting at lunch in the Blue Cat, Poirot finished outlining his instructions to Maude Williams.

'So you understand what it is you have to look for?'

Maude Williams nodded.

'You have arranged matters with your office?'

She laughed.

'My auntie's dangerously ill! I sent myself a telegram.'

'Good. I have one more thing to say. Somewhere, in that village, we have a murderer at large. That is not a very safe thing to have.'

'Warning me?'

'Yes.'

'I can take care of myself,' said Maude Williams.

'That,' said Hercule Poirot, 'might be classed under the heading of Famous Last Words.'

She laughed again, a frank amused laugh. One or two heads at near tables turned around to look at her.

Poirot found himself appraising her carefully. A strong, confident young woman, full
of vitality, keyed up and eager to attempt a
dangerous task. Why? He thought again of
James Bentley, his gentle defeated voice, his
lifeless apathy. Nature was indeed curious
and interesting.

Maude said:

'You're *asking* me to do it, aren't you? Why
suddenly try to put me off?'

'Because if one offers a mission, one must
be exact about what it involves.'

'I don't think I'm in any danger,' said
Maude confidently.

'I do not think so at the moment. You are
unknown in Broadhinny?'

Maude considered.

'Ye-es. Yes, I should say so.'

'You have been there?'

'Once or twice — for the firm, of course
— only once recently — that was about five
months ago.'

'Who did you see? Where did you go?'

'I went to see an old lady — Mrs Carstairs
— or Carlisle — I can't remember her name
for sure. She was buying a small property
near here, and I went over to see her with
some papers and some queries and a
surveyor's report which we'd got for her.
She was staying at that Guest House sort of

place where you are.'

'Long Meadows?'

'That was it. Uncomfortable-looking house with a lot of dogs.'

Poirot nodded.

'Did you see Mrs Summerhayes, or Major Summerhayes?'

'I saw Mrs Summerhayes, I suppose it was. She took me up to the bedroom. The old pussy was in bed.'

'Would Mrs Summerhayes remember you?'

'Don't suppose so. Even if she did, it wouldn't matter, would it? After all, one changes one's job quite often these days. But I don't suppose she even looked at me. Her sort don't.'

There was a faint bitterness in Maude Williams' voice.

'Did you see anyone else in Broadhinny?'

Maude said rather awkwardly:

'Well, I saw Mr Bentley.'

'Ah, you saw Mr Bentley. By accident.'

Maude wriggled a little in her chair.

'No, as a matter of fact, I'd sent him a p.c. Telling him I was coming that day. Asked him if he'd meet me as a matter of fact. Not that there was anywhere to go. Dead little hole. No café or cinema or anything. 'S a matter of fact we just talked in the bus stop. While I was waiting for my bus back.'

'That was before the death of Mrs McGinty?'

'Oh yes. But not much before, though. Because it was only a few days later that it was in all the newspapers.'

'Did Mr Bentley speak to you at all of his landlady?'

'I don't think so.'

'And you spoke to no one else in Broadhinny?'

'Well — only Mr Robin Upward. I've heard him talk on the wireless. I saw him coming out of his cottage and I recognized him from his pictures and I did ask him for his autograph.'

'And he gave it to you?'

'Oh yes, he was ever so nice about it. I hadn't my book with me, but I'd got an odd sheet of notepaper, and he whipped out his fountain pen and wrote it at once.'

'Do you know any of the other people in Broadhinny by sight?'

'Well, I know the Carpenters, of course. They're in Kilchester a lot. Lovely car they've got, and she wears lovely clothes. She opened a Bazaar about a month ago. They say he's going to be our next M.P.'

Poirot nodded. Then he took from his pocket the envelope that he always carried about with him. He spread the four photographs on the table.

'Do you recognize any of — what's the matter?'

'It was Mr Scuttle. Just going out of the door. I hope he didn't see you with me. It might seem a bit odd. People are talking about you, you know. Saying you've been sent over from Paris — from the Sooretay or some name like that.'

'I am Belgian, not French, but no matter.'

'What's this about these photographs?' She bent over, studying them closely. 'Rather on the old-fashioned side, aren't they?'

'The oldest is thirty years ago.'

'Awfully silly, old-fashioned clothes look. Makes the women look such fools.'

'Have you seen any of them before?'

'D'you mean do I recognize any of the women, or do you mean have I seen the pictures?'

'Either.'

'I've an idea I've seen that one.' Her finger rested against Janice Courtland in her cloche hat. 'In some paper or other, but I can't remember when. That kid looks a bit familiar, too. But I can't remember when I saw them; some time ago.'

'All those photographs appeared in the *Sunday Comet* on the Sunday before Mrs McGinty died.'

216

Maude looked at him sharply.

'And they've got something to do with it? That's why you want me to — '

She did not finish the sentence.

'Yes,' said Hercule Poirot. 'That is why.'

He took something else from his pocket and showed it to her. It was the cutting from the *Sunday Comet*.

'You had better read that,' he said.

She read it carefully. Her bright golden head bent over the flimsy bit of newsprint.

Then she looked up.

'So that's who they are? And reading this has given you ideas?'

'You could not express it more justly.'

'But all the same I don't see — ' She was silent a moment, thinking. Poirot did not speak. However pleased he might be with his own ideas, he was always ready to hear other people's ideas too.

'You think one or other of these people is in Broadhinny?'

'It might be, might it not?'

'Of course. Anyone may be anywhere . . . ' She went on, placing her finger on Eva Kane's pretty simpering face: 'She'd be quite old now — about Mrs Upward's age.'

'About that.'

'What I was thinking was — the sort of woman she was — there must be several people who'd have it in for her.'

'That is a point of view,' said Poirot slowly. 'Yes, it is a point of view.' He added: 'You remember the Craig case?'

'Who doesn't?' said Maude Williams. 'Why, he's in Madame Tussaud's! I was only a kid at the time, but the newspapers are always bringing him up and comparing the case with other cases. I don't suppose it will ever be forgotten, do you?'

Poirot raised his head sharply.

He wondered what brought that sudden note of bitterness into her voice.

17

Feeling completely bewildered, Mrs Oliver was endeavouring to cower in the corner of a very minute theatrical dressing-room. Not being the figure to cower, she only succeeded in bulging. Bright young men, removing grease paint with towels, surrounded her and at intervals pressed warm beer upon her.

Mrs Upward, her good humour completely restored, had speeded their departure with good wishes, Robin had been assiduous in making all arrangements for her comfort before departure, running back a couple of times after they were in the car to see that all was as it should be.

On the last occasion he came back grinning.

'Madre was just ringing off on the telephone, and the wicked old thing still won't tell me who she was ringing up. But I bet I know.'

'I know, too,' said Mrs Oliver.

'Well, who do you say?'

'Hercule Poirot.'

'Yes, that's my guess, too. She's going to pump him, Madre does like having her little secrets, doesn't she? Now darling, about the play tonight. It's very important that you tell me honestly just what you think of Cecil — and whether he's your idea of Eric . . . '

Needless to say, Cecil Leech had not been at all Mrs Oliver's idea of Eric. Nobody, indeed, could have been more unlike. The play itself she had enjoyed, but the ordeal of 'going round afterwards' was fraught with its usual terrors.

Robin, of course, was in his element. He had Cecil (at least Mrs Oliver supposed it was Cecil) pinned against the wall and was talking nineteen to the dozen. Mrs Oliver had been terrified of Cecil and much preferred somebody called Michael who was talking to her kindly at the moment. Michael, at least, did not expect her to reciprocate, in fact Michael seemed to prefer a monologue. Somebody called Peter made occasional incursions on the conversation, but on the whole it resolved itself into a stream of faintly amusing malice by Michael.

' — too sweet of Robin,' he was saying. 'We've been urging him to come and see the show. But of course he's completely under that terrible woman's thumb, isn't he? Dancing attendance. And really Robin is brilliant, don't you think so? Quite quite brilliant. He shouldn't be sacrificed on a

Matriarchal altar. Women can be awful, can't they? You know what she did to poor Alex Roscoff? All over him for nearly a year and then discovered that he wasn't a Russian émigré at all. Of course he had been telling her some very tall stories, but quite amusing, and we all knew it wasn't true, but after all why should one care? — and then when she found out he was just a little East End tailor's son, she dropped him, my dear. I mean, I do hate a snob, don't you? Really Alex was thankful to get away from her. He said she could be quite frightening sometimes — a little queer in the head, he thought. Her rages! Robin dear, we're talking about your wonderful Madre. Such a shame she couldn't come tonight. But it's marvellous to have Mrs Oliver. All those delicious murders.'

An elderly man with a deep bass voice grasped Mrs Oliver's hand and held it in a hot, sticky grasp.

'How can I ever thank you?' he said in tones of deep melancholy. 'You've saved my life — saved my life many a time.'

Then they all came out into the fresh night air and went across to the Pony's Head, where there were more drinks and more stage conversation.

By the time Mrs Oliver and Robin were driving homeward, Mrs Oliver was quite exhausted. She leaned back and closed her eyes. Robin, on the other hand, talked without stopping.

' — and you do think that might be an idea, don't you?' he finally ended.

'What?'

Mrs Oliver jerked open her eyes.

She had been lost in a nostalgic dream of home. Walls covered with exotic birds and foliage. A deal table, her typewriter, black coffee, apples everywhere . . . What bliss, what glorious and solitary bliss! What a mistake for an author to emerge from her secret fastness. Authors were shy, unsociable creatures, atoning for their lack of social aptitude by inventing their own companions and conversations.

'I'm afraid you're tired,' said Robin.

'Not really. The truth is I'm not very good with people.'

'I adore people, don't you?' said Robin happily.

'No,' said Mrs Oliver firmly.

'But you must. Look at all the people in your books.'

'That's different. I think trees are much nicer than people, more restful.'

'I need people,' said Robin, stating an obvious fact. 'They stimulate me.'

He drew up at the gate of Laburnums.

'You go in,' he said. 'I'll put the car away.'

Mrs Oliver extracted herself with the usual difficulty and walked up the path.

'The door's not locked,' Robin called.

It wasn't. Mrs Oliver pushed it open and entered. There were no lights on, and that struck her as rather ungracious on the hostess's part. Or was it perhaps economy? Rich people were so often economical. There was a smell of scent in the hall, something rather exotic and expensive. For a moment Mrs Oliver wondered if she were in the right house, then she found the light switch and pressed it down.

The light sprang up in the low oak-beamed square hall. The door into the sitting-room was ajar and she caught sight of a foot and leg. Mrs Upward, after all, had not gone to bed. She must have fallen asleep in her chair, and since no lights were on, she must have been asleep a long time.

Mrs Oliver went to the door and switched on the lights in the sitting-room.

'We're back — ' she began and then stopped.

Her hand went up to her throat. She felt a tight knot there, a desire to scream that she could not put into operation.

Her voice came out in a whisper:

'Robin — Robin . . .'

It was some time before she heard him coming up the path, whistling, and then she turned quickly and ran to meet him in the hall.

'Don't go in there — don't go in. Your mother — she — she's dead — I think — she's been killed . . . '

18

I

'Quite a neat bit of work,' said Superintendent Spence.

His red countryman's face was angry. He looked across to where Hercule Poirot sat gravely listening.

'Neat and ugly,' he said. 'She was strangled,' he went on. 'Silk scarf — one of her own silk scarves, one she'd been wearing that day — just passed around the neck and the ends crossed — and pulled. Neat, quick, efficient. The thugs did it that way in India. The victim doesn't struggle or cry out — pressure on the carotid artery.'

'Special knowledge?'

'Could be — need not. If you were thinking of doing it, you could read up the subject. There's no practical difficulty. 'Specially with the victim quite unsuspicious — and she *was* unsuspicious.'

Poirot nodded.

'Someone she knew.'

'Yes. They had coffee together — a cup

225

opposite her and one opposite the — guest. Prints had been wiped off the guest's cup very carefully but lipstick is more difficult — there were still faint traces of lipstick.'

'A woman, then?'

'You expected a woman, didn't you?'

'Oh yes. Yes, that was indicated.'

Spence went on:

'Mrs Upward recognized one of those photographs — the photograph of Lily Gamboll. So it ties up with the McGinty murder.'

'Yes,' said Poirot. 'It ties up with the McGinty murder.'

He remembered Mrs Upward's slightly amused expression as she had said:

'Mrs McGinty's dead. How did she die?
Sticking her neck out, just like I.'

Spence was going on:

'She took an opportunity that seemed good to her — her son and Mrs Oliver were going off to the theatre. She rang up the person concerned and asked that person to come and see her. Is that how you figure it out? She was playing detective.'

'Something like that. Curiosity. She kept her knowledge to herself, but she wanted to find out more. She didn't in the least realize what she was doing might be dangerous.' Poirot sighed. 'So many people think of murder as a game. It is not a game. I told her so. But she would not listen.'

'No, we know that. Well, that fits in fairly well. When young Robin started off with Mrs Oliver and ran back into the house his mother had just finished telephoning to someone. She wouldn't say who to. Played it mysterious. Robin and Mrs Oliver thought it might be *you*.'

'I wish it had been,' said Hercule Poirot. 'You have no idea to whom it was that she telephoned?'

'None whatever. It's all automatic round here, you know.'

'The maid couldn't help you in any way?'

'No. She came in about half-past ten — she has a key to the back door. She went straight into her own room which leads off the kitchen and went to bed. The house was dark and she assumed that Mrs Upward had gone to bed and that the others had not yet returned.'

Spence added:

'She's deaf and pretty crotchety as well. Takes very little notice of what goes on — and I imagine does as little work as she can with as much grumbling as possible.'

'Not really an old faithful?'

'Oh no! She's only been with the Upwards a couple of years.'

A constable put his head round the door.

'There's a young lady to see you, sir,' he said. 'Says there's something perhaps you ought to know. About last night.'

'About last night? Send her in.'

Deirdre Henderson came in. She looked pale and strained and, as usual, rather awkward.

'I thought perhaps I'd better come,' she said. 'If I'm not interrupting you or anything,' she added apologetically.

'Not at all, Miss Henderson.'

Spence rose and pushed forward a chair. She sat down on it squarely in an ungainly schoolgirlish sort of way.

'Something about last night?' said Spence encouragingly. 'About Mrs Upward, you mean?'

'Yes, it's true, isn't it, that she was murdered? I mean the post said so and the baker. Mother said of course it couldn't be true — ' She stopped.

'I'm afraid your mother isn't quite right there. It's true enough. Now, you wanted to make a — to tell us something?'

Deirdre nodded.

'Yes,' she said. 'You see, *I* was there.'

A difference crept into Spence's manner. It

was, perhaps, even more gentle, but an official hardness underlay it.

'You were there,' he said. 'At Laburnums. At what time?'

'I don't know exactly,' said Deirdre. 'Between half-past eight and nine, I suppose. Probably nearly nine. After dinner, anyway. You see, she telephoned to me.'

'Mrs Upward telephoned to you?'

'Yes. She said Robin and Mrs Oliver were going to the theatre in Cullenquay and that she would be all alone and would I come along and have coffee with her.'

'And you went?'

'Yes.'

'And you — had coffee with her?'

Deirdre shook her head.

'No, I got there — and I knocked. But there wasn't any answer. So I opened the door and went into the hall. It was quite dark and I'd seen from outside that there was no light in the sitting-room. So I was puzzled. I called 'Mrs Upward' once or twice but there was no answer. So I thought there must be some mistake.'

'What mistake did you think there could have been?'

'I thought perhaps she'd gone to the theatre with them after all.'

'Without letting you know?'

'That did seem queer.'

'You couldn't think of any other explanation?'

'Well, I thought perhaps Frieda might have bungled the original message. She does get things wrong sometimes. She's a foreigner. She was excited herself last night because she was leaving.'

'What did you do, Miss Henderson?'

'I just went away.'

'Back home?'

'Yes — that is, I went for a walk first. It was quite fine.'

Spence was silent for a moment or two, looking at her. He was looking, Poirot noticed, at her mouth.

Presently he roused himself and said briskly:

'Well, thank you, Miss Henderson. You were quite right to come and tell us this. We're much obliged to you.'

He got up and shook hands with her.

'I thought I ought to,' said Deirdre. 'Mother didn't want me to.'

'Didn't she now?'

'But I thought I'd better.'

'Quite right.'

He showed her out and came back.

He sat down, drummed on the table and looked at Poirot.

'No lipstick,' he said. 'Or is that only this morning?'

'No, it is not only this morning. She never uses it.'

'That's odd, nowadays, isn't it?'

'She is rather an odd kind of girl — undeveloped.'

'And no scent, either, as far as I could smell. That Mrs Oliver says there was a distinct smell of scent — expensive scent, she says — in the house last night. Robin Upward confirms that. It wasn't any scent his mother uses.'

'This girl would not use scent, I think,' said Poirot.

'I shouldn't think so either,' said Spence. 'Looks rather like the hockey captain from an old-fashioned girls' school — but she must be every bit of thirty, I should say.'

'Quite that.'

'Arrested development, would you say?'

Poirot considered. Then he said it was not quite so simple as that.

'It doesn't fit,' said Spence frowning. 'No lipstick, no scent. And since she's got a perfectly good mother, and Lily Gamboll's mother was done in in a drunken brawl in Cardiff when Lily Gamboll was nine years old, I don't see how she can be Lily Gamboll. *But* — Mrs Upward telephoned her to come

231

there last night — you can't get away from that.' He rubbed his nose. 'It isn't straightforward going.'

'What about the medical evidence?'

'Not much help there. All the police surgeon will say definitely is that she was probably dead by half-past nine.'

'So she may have been dead when Deirdre Henderson came to Laburnums?'

'Probably was if the girl is speaking the truth. Either she *is* speaking the truth — or else she's a deep one. Mother didn't want her to come to us, she said. Anything there?'

Poirot considered.

'Not particularly. It is what mother would say. She is the type, you comprehend, that avoids unpleasantness.'

Spence sighed.

'So we've got Deirdre Henderson — on the spot. Or else someone who came there before Deirdre Henderson. A woman. A woman who used lipstick and expensive scent.'

Poirot murmured: 'You will inquire — '

Spence broke in.

'I'm inquiring! Just tactfully for the moment. We don't want to alarm anyone. What was Eve Carpenter doing last night? What was Shelagh Rendell doing last night? Ten to one they were just sitting at home. Carpenter, I know, had a political meeting.'

'Eve,' said Poirot thoughtfully. 'The fashions in names change, do they not? Hardly ever, nowadays, do you hear of an Eva. It has gone out. But Eve, it is popular.'

'She can afford expensive scent,' said Spence, pursuing his own train of thought.

He sighed.

'We've got to get at more of her background. It's so convenient to be a war widow. You can turn up anywhere looking pathetic and mourning some brave young airman. Nobody likes to ask you questions.

He turned to another subject.

'That sugar hammer or what-not you sent along — I think you've hit the bull's-eye. It's the weapon used in the McGinty murder. Doctor agrees it's exactly suitable for the type of blow. And there has been blood on it. It was washed, of course — but they don't realize nowadays that a microscopic amount of blood will give a reaction with the latest reagents. Yes, it's human blood all right. And that again ties up with the Wetherbys and the Henderson girl. Or doesn't it?'

'Deirdre Henderson was quite definite that the sugar hammer went to the Harvest Festival Bring and Buy.'

'And Mrs Summerhayes was equally positive it was the Christmas one?'

'Mrs Summerhayes is never positive about

anything,' said Poirot gloomily. 'She is a charming person, but she has no order or method in her composition. But I will tell you this — I who have lived at Long Meadows — the doors and the windows they are always open. Anyone — anyone at all, could come and take something away and later come and put it back and neither Major Summerhayes nor Mrs Summerhayes would notice. If it is not there one day, she thinks that her husband has taken it to joint a rabbit or to chop wood — and he, he would think she had taken it to chop dogmeat. In that house nobody uses the right implements — they just seize what is at hand and leave it in the wrong place. And nobody remembers anything. If I were to live like that I should be in a continual state of anxiety — but they — they do not seem to mind.'

Spence sighed.

'Well — there's one good thing about all this — they won't execute James Bentley until this business is all cleared up. We've forwarded a letter to the Home Secretary's office. It gives us what we've been wanting — time.'

'I think,' said Poirot, 'that I would like to see Bentley again — now that we know a little more.'

II

There was little change in James Bentley. He was, perhaps, rather thinner, his hands were more restless — otherwise he was the same quiet, hopeless creature.

Hercule Poirot spoke carefully. There had been some fresh evidence. The police were re-opening the case. There was, therefore, hope . . .

But James Bentley was not attracted by hope.

He said:

'It will be all no good. What more can they find out?'

'Your friends,' said Hercule Poirot, 'are working very hard.'

'My friends?' He shrugged his shoulders. 'I have no friends.'

'You should not say that. You have, at the very least, two friends.'

'Two friends? I should like to know who they are.'

His tone expressed no wish for the information, merely a weary disbelief.

'First, there is Superintendent Spence — '

'Spence? Spence? The police superintendent who worked up the case against me? That's almost funny.'

'It is not funny. It is fortunate. Spence is a

very shrewd and conscientious police officer. He likes to be very sure that he has got the right man.'

'He's sure enough of that.'

'Oddly enough, he is not. That is why, as I said, he is your friend.'

'That kind of a friend!'

Hercule Poirot waited. Even James Bentley, he thought, must have some human attributes. Even James Bentley could not be completely devoid of ordinary human curiosity.

And true enough, presently James Bentley said:

'Well, who's the other?'

'The other is Maude Williams.'

Bentley did not appear to react.

'Maude Williams? Who is she?'

'She worked in the office of Breather & Scuttle.'

'Oh — that Miss Williams.'

'*Précisément*, that Miss Williams.'

'But what's it got to do with her?'

There were moments when Hercule Poirot found the personality of James Bentley so irritating that he heartily wished that he could believe Bentley guilty of Mrs McGinty's murder. Unfortunately the more Bentley annoyed him, the more he came round to Spence's way of thinking. He found it more and more difficult to envisage Bentley's murdering anybody. James Bentley's attitude to murder would have been, Poirot felt sure, that it wouldn't be much good anyway. If cockiness, as Spence insisted, was a characteristic of murderers, Bentley was certainly no murderer.

Containing himself, Poirot said:

'Miss Williams interests herself in this affair. She is convinced you are innocent.'

'I don't see what she can know about it.'

'She knows *you*.'

James Bentley blinked. He said, grudgingly:

'I suppose she does, in a way, but not well.'

'You worked together in the office, did you not? You had, sometimes, meals together?'

'Well — yes — once or twice. The Blue Cat Café, it's very convenient — just across the street.'

'Did you never go for walks with her?'

'As a matter of fact we did, once. We walked up on the downs.'

Hercule Poirot exploded.

'*Ma foi*, is it a crime that I seek to drag from you? To keep the company with a pretty girl, is it not natural? Is it not enjoyable? Can you not be pleased with yourself about it?'

'I don't see why,' said James Bentley.

'At your age it is natural and right to enjoy

the company of girls.'

'I don't know many girls.'

'*Ça se voit!* But you should be ashamed of that, not smug! You knew Miss Williams. You had worked with her and talked with her and sometimes had meals with her, and once went for a walk on the downs. And when I mention her, you do not even remember her name!'

James Bentley flushed.

'Well, you see — I've never had much to do with girls. And she isn't quite what you'd call a lady, is she? Oh very nice — and all that — but I can't help feeling that Mother would have thought her common.'

'It is what *you* think that matters.'

Again James Bentley flushed.

'Her hair,' he said. 'And the kind of clothes she wears — Mother, of course, was old-fashioned — '

He broke off.

'But you found Miss Williams — what shall I say — sympathetic?'

'She was always very kind,' said James Bentley slowly. 'But she didn't — really — *understand*. Her mother died when she was only a child, you see.'

'And then you lost your job,' said Poirot. 'You couldn't get another. Miss Williams met you once at Broadhinny, I understand?'

James Bentley looked distressed.

'Yes — yes. She was coming over there on business and she sent me a post-card. Asked me to meet her. I can't think why. It isn't as if I knew her at all well.'

'But you did meet her?'

'Yes. I didn't want to be rude.'

'And you took her to the pictures or a meal?'

James Bentley looked scandalized.

'Oh no. Nothing of that kind. We — er — just talked whilst she was waiting for her bus.'

'Ah, how amusing that must have been for the poor girl!'

James Bentley said sharply:

'I hadn't got any money. You must remember that. I hadn't any money at all.'

'Of course. It was a few days before Mrs McGinty was killed, wasn't it?'

James Bentley nodded. He said unexpectedly:

'Yes, it was on the Monday. She was killed on Wednesday.'

'I'm going to ask you something else, Mr Bentley. Mrs McGinty took the *Sunday Comet*?'

'Yes, she did.'

'Did you ever see her *Sunday Comet*?'

'She used to offer it sometimes, but I didn't

239

often accept. Mother didn't care for that kind of paper.'

'So you didn't see that week's *Sunday Comet*?'

'No.'

'And Mrs McGinty didn't speak about it, or about anything in it?'

'Oh yes, she did,' said James Bentley unexpectedly. 'She was full of it!'

'Ah la la. So she was full of it. And what did she say? Be careful. This is important.'

'I don't remember very well now. It was all about some old murder case. Craig, I think it was — no, perhaps it wasn't Craig. Anyway, she said somebody connected with the case was living in Broadhinny now. Full of it, she was. I couldn't see why it mattered to her.'

'Did she say who it was — in Broadhinny?'

James Bentley said vaguely:

'I think it was that woman whose son writes plays.'

'She mentioned her by name?'

'No — I — really it's so long ago — '

'I implore you — try to think. You want to be free again, do you not?'

'Free?' Bentley sounded surprised.

'Yes, free.'

'I — yes — I suppose I do — '

'Then *think! What did Mrs McGinty say*?'

'Well — something like — 'so pleased with herself as she is and so proud. Not so much to be proud of if all's known.' And then, 'You'd never think it was the same woman to look at the photograph.' But of course it had been taken years ago.'

'But what made you sure that it was Mrs Upward of whom she was speaking?'

'I really don't know . . . I just formed the impression. She had been speaking of Mrs Upward — and then I lost interest and didn't listen, and afterwards — well, now I come to think of it, I don't really know who she was speaking about. She talked a lot you know.'

Poirot sighed.

He said: 'I do not think myself that it was Mrs Upward of whom she spoke. I think it was somebody else. It is preposterous to reflect that if you are hanged it will be because you do not pay proper attention to the people with whom you converse . . . Did Mrs McGinty speak much to you of the houses where she worked, or the ladies of those houses?'

'Yes, in a way — but it's no good asking me. You don't seem to realize, M. Poirot, that I had my own life to think of at the time. I was in very serious anxiety.'

'Not in so much serious anxiety as you are

now! Did Mrs McGinty speak of Mrs Carpenter — Mrs Selkirk she was then — or of Mrs Rendell?'

'Carpenter has that new house at the top of the hill and a big car, hasn't he? He was engaged to Mrs Selkirk — Mrs McGinty was always very down on Mrs Selkirk. I don't know why. 'Jumped up', that's what she used to call her. I don't know what she meant by it.'

'And the Rendells?'

'He's the doctor, isn't he? I don't remember her saying anything particular about them.'

'And the Wetherbys?'

'I do remember what she said about them. 'No patience with her fusses and her fancies,' that's what she said. And about him, 'Never a word, good or bad, out of him.' ' He paused. 'She said — it was an unhappy house.'

Hercule Poirot looked up. For a second James Bentley's voice had held something that Poirot had not heard in it before. He was not repeating obediently what he could recall. His mind, for a very brief space, had moved out of its apathy. James Bentley was thinking of Hunter's Close, of the life that went on there, of whether or not it was an unhappy house. James Bentley was thinking objectively.

Poirot said softly:

'You knew them? The mother? The father? The daughter?'

'Not really. It was the dog. A Sealyham. It got caught in a trap. She couldn't get it undone. I helped her.'

There was again something new in Bentley's tone. 'I helped her,' he had said, and in those words was a faint echo of pride.

Poirot remembered what Mrs Oliver had told him of her conversation with Deirdre Henderson.

He said gently:

'You talked together?'

'Yes. She — her mother suffered a lot, she told me. She was very fond of her mother.'

'And you told her about yours?'

'Yes,' said James Bentley simply.

Poirot said nothing. He waited.

'Life is very cruel,' said James Bentley. 'Very unfair. Some people never seem to get any happiness.'

'It is possible,' said Hercule Poirot.

'I don't think she had had much. Miss Wetherby.'

'Henderson.'

'Oh yes. She told me she had a stepfather.'

'Deirdre Henderson,' said Poirot. 'Deirdre

of the Sorrows. A pretty name — but not a pretty girl, I understand?'

James Bentley flushed.

'*I* thought,' he said, 'she was rather good-looking . . . '

19

'Now just you listen to me,' said Mrs Sweetiman.

Edna sniffed. She had been listening to Mrs Sweetiman for some time. It had been a hopeless conversation, going round in circles. Mrs Sweetiman had said the same thing several times, varying the phraseology a little, but even that not much. Edna had sniffed and occasionally blubbered and had reiterated her own two contributions to the discussion: first, that she couldn't ever! Second, that Dad would skin her alive, he would.

'That's as may be,' said Mrs Sweetiman, 'but murder's murder, and what you saw you saw, and you can't get away from it.'

Edna sniffed.

'And what you did ought to do — '

Mrs Sweetiman broke off and attended to Mrs Wetherby, who had come in for some knitting pins and another ounce of wool.

'Haven't seen you about for some time, ma'am,' said Mrs Sweetiman brightly.

'No, I've been very far from well lately,' said Mrs Wetherby. 'My heart, you know.' She sighed deeply. 'I have to lie up a great deal.'

'I heard as you've got some help at last,' said Mrs Sweetiman. 'You'll want dark needles for this light wool.'

'Yes. Quite capable as far as she goes, and cooks not at all badly. But her manners! And her appearance! Dyed hair and the most unsuitable tight jumpers.'

'Ah,' said Mrs Sweetiman. 'Girls aren't trained proper to service nowadays. My mother, she started at thirteen and she got up at a quarter to five every morning. Head housemaid she was when she finished, and three maids under her. And she trained them proper, too. But there's none of that nowadays — girls aren't trained nowadays, they're just educated, like Edna.'

Both women looked at Edna, who leant against the post office counter, sniffing and sucking a peppermint, and looking particularly vacant. As an example of education, she hardly did the educational system credit.

'Terrible about Mrs Upward, wasn't it?' continued Mrs Sweetiman conversationally, as Mrs Wetherby sorted through various coloured needles.

'Dreadful,' said Mrs Wetherby. 'They hardly dared tell me. And when they did, I had the most frightful palpitations. I'm so sensitive.'

'Shock to all of us, it was,' said Mrs Sweetiman. 'As for young Mr Upward, he took on something terrible. Had her hands full with him, the authoress lady did, until the doctor came and gave him a seddytiff or something. He's gone up to Long Meadows now as a paying guest, felt he couldn't stay in the cottage — and I don't know as I blame him. Janet Groom, she's gone home to her niece and the police have got the key. The lady what writes the murder books has gone back to London, but she'll come down for the inquest.'

Mrs Sweetiman imparted all this information with relish. She prided herself on being well informed. Mrs Wetherby, whose desire for knitting needles had perhaps been prompted by a desire to know what was going on, paid for her purchase.

'It's most upsetting,' she said. 'It makes the whole village so *dangerous*. There must be a maniac about. When I think that my own dear daughter was out that night, that she herself might have been attacked, perhaps killed.' Mrs Wetherby closed both eyes and swayed on her feet. Mrs Sweetiman watched her with interest, but without alarm. Mrs Wetherby opened her eyes again, and said with dignity:

'This place should be patrolled. No young people should go about after dark. And all doors should be locked and bolted. You know that up at Long Meadows, Mrs Summerhayes never locks *any* of her doors. Not even at *night*. She leaves the back door and the drawing-room window open so that the dogs and cats can get in and out. I myself consider that is absolute madness, but she says they've always done it and that if burglars want to get in, they always can.'

'Reckon there wouldn't be much for a burglar to take up at Long Meadows,' said Mrs Sweetiman.

Mrs Wetherby shook her head sadly and departed with her purchase.

Mrs Sweetiman and Edna resumed their argument.

'It's no good your setting yourself up to know best,' said Mrs Sweetiman. 'Right's right and murder's murder. Tell the truth and shame the devil. That's what I say.'

'Dad would skin me alive, he would, for sure,' said Edna.

'I'd talk to your Dad,' said Mrs Sweetiman.

'I couldn't ever,' said Edna.

'Mrs Upward's dead,' said Mrs Sweetiman. 'And you saw something the police don't know about. You're employed in the post office, aren't you? You're a Government servant. You've got to do your duty. You've got to go along to Bert Hayling — '

Edna's sobs burst out anew.

'Not to Bert, I couldn't. However could I go to Bert? It'd be all over the place.'

Mrs Sweetiman said rather hesitantly:

'There's that foreign gentleman — '

'Not a foreigner, I couldn't. Not a foreigner.'

'No, maybe you're right there.'

A car drew up outside the post office with a squealing of brakes.

Mrs Sweetiman's face lit up.

'That's Major Summerhayes, that is. You tell it all to him and he'll advise you what to do.'

'I couldn't ever,' said Edna, but with less conviction.

Johnnie Summerhayes came into the post office, staggering under the burden of three cardboard boxes.

'Good morning, Mrs Sweetiman,' he said cheerfully. 'Hope these aren't overweight?'

Mrs Sweetiman attended to the parcels in her official capacity. As Summerhayes was licking the stamps, she spoke.

'Excuse me, sir, I'd like your advice about something.'

'Yes, Mrs Sweetiman?'

'Seeing as you belong here, sir, and will know best what to do.'

Summerhayes nodded. He was always

curiously touched by the lingering feudal spirit of English villages. The villagers knew little of him personally, but because his father and his grandfather and many great-great-grandfathers had lived at Long Meadows, they regarded it as natural that he should advise and direct them when asked so to do.

'It's about Edna here,' said Mrs Sweetiman.

Edna sniffed.

Johnnie Summerhayes looked at Edna doubtfully. Never, he thought, had he seen a more unprepossessing girl. Exactly like a skinned rabbit. Seemed half-witted too. Surely she couldn't be in what was known officially as 'trouble'. But no, Mrs Sweetiman would not have come to him for advice in that case.

'Well,' he said kindly, 'what's the difficulty?'

'It's about the murder, sir. The night of the murder. Edna saw something.'

Johnnie Summerhayes transferred his quick dark gaze from Edna to Mrs Sweetiman and back again to Edna.

'What did you see, Edna?' he said.

Edna began to sob. Mrs Sweetiman took over.

'Of course we've been hearing this and that. Some's rumour and some's true. But it's said definite as that there were a lady there that night who drank coffee with Mrs Upward. That's so, isn't it, sir?'

'Yes, I believe so.'

'I know as that's true, because we had it from Bert Hayling.'

Albert Hayling was the local constable whom Summerhayes knew well. A slow-speaking man with a sense of his own importance.

'I see,' said Summerhayes.

'But they don't know, do they, who the lady is? Well, Edna here *saw* her.'

Johnnie Summerhayes looked at Edna. He pursed his lips as though to whistle.

'You saw her, did you, Edna? Going in — or coming out?'

'Going in,' said Edna. A faint sense of importance loosened her tongue. 'Across the road I was, under the trees. Just by the turn of the lane where it's dark. I saw her. She went in at the gate and up to the door and she stood there a bit, and then — and then she went in.'

Johnnie Summerhayes' brow cleared.

'That's all right,' he said. 'It was Miss Henderson. The police know all about that. She went and told them.'

Edna shook her head.

'It wasn't Miss Henderson,' she said.

'It wasn't — then who was it?'

'I dunno. I didn't see her face. Had her back to me, she had, going up the path and standing there. But it wasn't Miss Henderson.'

'But how do you know it wasn't Miss Henderson if you didn't see her face?'

'Because she had fair hair. Miss Henderson's is dark.'

Johnnie Summerhayes looked disbelieving.

'It was a very dark night. You'd hardly be able to see the colour of anyone's hair.'

'But I did, though. That light was on over the porch. Left like that, it was, because Mr Robin and the detective lady had gone out together to the theatre. And she was standing right under it. A dark coat she had on, and no hat, and her hair was shining fair as could be. I saw it.'

Johnnie gave a slow whistle. His eyes were serious now.

'What time was it?' he asked.

Edna sniffed.

'I don't rightly know.'

'You know about what time,' said Mrs Sweetiman.

'It wasn't nine o'clock. I'd have heard the church. And it was after half-past eight.'

'Between half-past eight and nine. How long did she stop?'

'I dunno, sir. Because I didn't wait no

longer. And I didn't hear nothing. No groans or cries or nothing like that.'

Edna sounded slightly aggrieved.

But there would have been no groans and no cries. Johnnie Summerhayes knew that. He said gravely:

'Well, there's only one thing to be done. The police have got to hear about this.'

Edna burst into long sniffling sobs.

'Dad'll skin me alive,' she whimpered. 'He will, for sure.'

She cast an imploring look at Mrs Sweetiman and bolted into the back room. Mrs Sweetiman took over with competence.

'It's like this, sir,' she said in answer to Summerhayes' inquiring glance. 'Edna's been behaving very foolish like. Very strict her Dad is, maybe a bit over strict, but it's hard to say what's best nowadays. There's a nice young fellow over to Cullavon and he and Edna have been going together nice and steady, and her Dad was quite pleased about it, but Reg he's on the slow side, and you know what girls are. Edna's taken up lately with Charlie Masters.'

'Masters? One of Farmer Cole's men, isn't he?'

'That's right, sir. Farm labourer. And a married man with two children. Always after the girls, he is, and a bad fellow in every way.

Edna hasn't got any sense, and her Dad, he put a stop to it. Quite right. So, you see, Edna was going into Cullavon that night to go to the pictures with Reg — at least that's what she told her Dad. But really she went out to meet this Masters. Waited for him, she did, at the turn of the lane where it seems they used to meet. Well, he didn't come. Maybe his wife kept him at home, or maybe he's after another girl, but there it is. Edna waited but at last she gave up. But it's awkward for her, as you can see, explaining what she was doing there, when she ought to have taken the bus into Cullavon.'

Johnnie Summerhayes nodded. Suppressing an irrelevant feeling of wonder that the unprepossessing Edna could have sufficient sex appeal to attract the attention of two men, he dealt with the practical aspect of the situation.

'She doesn't want to go to Bert Hayling about it,' he said with quick comprehension.

'That's right, sir.'

Summerhayes reflected rapidly.

'I'm afraid the police have got to know,' he said gently.

'That's what I told her, sir,' said Mrs Sweetiman.

'But they will probably be quite tactful about — er — the circumstances. Possibly she mayn't have to give evidence. And what she tells them, they'll keep to themselves. I could ring up Spence and ask him to come over here — no, better still, I'll take young Edna into Kilchester with me in my car. If she goes to the police station there, nobody here need know anything about it. I'll just ring them up first and warn them we're coming.'

And so, after a brief telephone call, the sniffing Edna, buttoned firmly into her coat and encouraged by a pat on the back from Mrs Sweetiman, stepped into the station wagon and was driven rapidly away in the direction of Kilchester.

20

Hercule Poirot was in Superintendent Spence's office in Kilchester. He was leaning back in a chair, his eyes closed and the tips of his fingers just touching each other in front of him.

The superintendent received some reports, gave instructions to a sergeant, and finally looked across at the other man.

'Getting a brainwave, M. Poirot?' he demanded.

'I reflect,' said Poirot. 'I review.'

'I forgot to ask you. Did you get anything useful from James Bentley when you saw him?'

Poirot shook his head. He frowned.

It was indeed of James Bentley he had been thinking.

It was annoying, thought Poirot with exasperation, that on a case such as this where he had offered his services without reward, solely out of friendship and respect for an upright police officer, that the victim of circumstances should so lack any romantic appeal. A lovely young girl, now, bewildered and innocent, or a fine upstanding young man, also bewildered, but whose 'head is bloody but unbowed,' thought Poirot, who had been reading a good deal of English poetry in an anthology lately. Instead, he had James Bentley, a pathological case if there ever was one, a self-centred creature who had never thought much of anyone but himself. A man ungrateful for the efforts that were being made to save him — almost, one might say, uninterested in them.

Really, thought Poirot, one might as well let him be hanged since he does not seem to care . . .

No, he would not go quite as far as that.

Superintendent Spence's voice broke into these reflections.

'Our interview,' said Poirot, 'was, if I might say so, singularly unproductive. Anything useful that Bentley might have remembered he did not remember — what he did remember is so vague and uncertain that one cannot build upon it. But at any rate it seems fairly certain that Mrs McGinty was excited by the article in the *Sunday Comet* and spoke about it to Bentley with special reference to 'someone connected with the case', living in Broadhinny.'

'With which case?' asked Superintendent Spence sharply.

'Our friend could not be sure,' said Poirot.

'He said, rather doubtfully, the Craig case — but the Craig case being the only one he had ever heard of, it would, presumably, be the only one he could remember. But the 'someone' was a woman. He even quoted Mrs McGinty's words. Someone who had 'not so much to be proud of if all's known'. '

'*Proud?*'

'*Mais oui,*' Poirot nodded his appreciation. 'A suggestive word, is it not?'

'No clue as to who the proud lady was?'

'Bentley suggested Mrs Upward — but as far as I can see for no real reason!'

Spence shook his head.

'Probably because she was a proud masterful sort of woman — outstandingly so, I should say. But it couldn't have been Mrs Upward, because Mrs Upward's dead, and dead for the same reason as Mrs McGinty died — because she recognized a photograph.'

Poirot said sadly: 'I warned her.'

Spence murmured irritably:

'Lily Gamboll! So far as age goes, there are only two possibilities, Mrs Rendell and Mrs Carpenter. I don't count the Henderson girl — she's got a background.'

'And the others have not?'

Spence sighed.

'You know what things are nowadays. The

war stirred up everyone and everything. The approved school where Lily Gamboll was, and all its records, were destroyed by a direct hit. Then take people. It's the hardest thing in the world to check on people. Take Broadhinny — the only people in Broadhinny we know anything about are the Summerhayes family, who have been there for three hundred years, and Guy Carpenter, who's one of the engineering Carpenters. All the others are — what shall I say — fluid? Dr Rendell's on the Medical Register and we know where he trained and where he's practised, but we don't know his home background. His wife came from near Dublin. Eve Selkirk, as she was before she married Guy Carpenter, was a pretty young war widow. Anyone can be a pretty young war widow. Take the Wetherbys — they seem to have floated round the world, here, there and everywhere. Why? Is there a reason? Did he embezzle from a bank? Or did they occasion a scandal? I don't say we can't dig up about people. We can — but it takes time. The people themselves won't help you.'

'Because they have something to conceal — but it need not be murder,' said Poirot.

'Exactly. It may be trouble with the law, or it may be a humble origin, or it may be common or garden scandal. But whatever it is, they've taken a lot of pains to cover up — and that makes it difficult to uncover.'

'But not impossible.'

'Oh no. Not impossible. It just takes time. As I say, if Lily Gamboll is in Broadhinny, she's *either* Eve Carpenter or Shelagh Rendell. I've questioned them — just routine — that's the way I put it. They say they were both at home — alone. Mrs Carpenter was the wide-eyed innocent, Mrs Rendell was nervous — but then she's a nervous type, you can't go by that.'

'Yes,' said Poirot thoughtfully. 'She is a nervous type.'

He was thinking of Mrs Rendell in the garden at Long Meadows. Mrs Rendell had received an anonymous letter, or so she said. He wondered, as he had wondered before, about that statement.

Spence went on:

'And we have to be careful — because even if one of them *is* guilty, the other is innocent.'

'And Guy Carpenter is a prospective Member of Parliament and an important local figure.'

'That wouldn't help him if he was guilty of murder or accessory to it,' said Spence grimly.

'I know that. But you have, have you not, to be *sure*?'

'That's right. Anyway, you'll agree, won't you, that it lies between the two of them?'

Poirot sighed.

'No — no — I would not say that. There are other possibilities.'

'Such as?'

Poirot was silent for a moment, then he said in a different, almost casual tone of voice:

'Why do people keep photographs?'

'Why? Goodness knows! Why do people keep all sorts of things — junk — trash, bits and pieces. They do — that's all there is to it!'

'Up to a point I agree with you. Some people keep things. Some people throw everything away as soon as they have done with it. That, yes, it is a matter of temperament. But I speak now especially of photographs. Why do people keep, in particular, *photographs?*'

'As I say, because they just don't throw things away. Or else because it reminds them — '

Poirot pounced on the words.

'Exactly. *It reminds them.* Now again we ask — why? *Why* does a woman keep a photograph of herself when young? And I say that the first reason is, essentially, vanity. She has been a pretty girl and she keeps a photograph of herself to remind her of what a pretty girl she was. It encourages her when her mirror tells her unpalatable things. She says, perhaps, to a friend, 'That was me when I was eighteen . . . ' and she sighs . . . You agree?'

'Yes — yes, I should say that's true enough.'

'Then that is reason No. 1. Vanity. Now reason No. 2. Sentiment.'

'That's the same thing?'

'No, no, not quite. Because this leads you to preserve not only your own photograph but that of someone else . . . A picture of your married daughter — when she was a child sitting on a hearthrug with tulle round her.'

'I've seen some of those,' Spence grinned.

'Yes. Very embarrassing to the subject sometimes, but mothers like to do it. And sons and daughters often keep pictures of their mothers, especially, say, if their mother died young. 'That was my mother as a girl.' '

'I'm beginning to see what you're driving at, Poirot.'

'And there is possibly, a *third* category. Not vanity, not sentiment, not love — perhaps *hate* — what do you say?'

'Hate?'

'Yes. To keep a desire for revenge alive. Someone who has injured you — you might keep a photograph to remind you, might you not?'

'But surely that doesn't apply in this case?'

'Does it not?'

'What are you thinking of?'

Poirot murmured:

'Newspaper reports are often inaccurate. The *Sunday Comet* stated that Eva Kane was employed by the Craigs as a nursery governess. Was that actually the case?'

'Yes, it was. But we're working on the assumption that it's Lily Gamboll we're looking for.'

Poirot sat up suddenly very straight in his chair. He wagged an imperative forefinger at Spence.

'Look. Look at the photograph of Lily Gamboll. She is not pretty — no! Frankly, with those teeth and those spectacles she is hideously ugly. Then nobody has kept that photograph for the first of our reasons. No woman would keep that photo out of vanity. If Eve Carpenter or Shelagh Rendell, who are both good-looking women, especially Eve Carpenter, had this photograph of themselves, they would tear it in pieces quickly in case somebody should see it!'

'Well, there is something in that.'

'So reason No. 1 is out. Now take sentiment. Did anybody love Lily Gamboll at that age? The whole point of Lily Gamboll is that they did not. She was an unwanted and unloved child. The person who liked her best was her aunt, and her aunt died under the chopper. So it was not sentiment that kept this picture. And revenge? Nobody hated her either. Her murdered aunt was a lonely woman without a husband and with no close friends. Nobody had hate for the little slum child — only pity.'

'Look here, M. Poirot, what you're saying is that *nobody* would have kept that photo.'

'Exactly — that is the result of my reflections.'

'But somebody did. Because Mrs Upward had seen it.'

'*Had she?*'

'Dash it all. It was you who told me. She said so herself.'

'Yes, she said so,' said Poirot. 'But the late Mrs Upward was, in some ways, a secretive woman. She liked to manage things her own way. I showed the photographs, and she recognized one of them. But then, for some reason, she wanted to keep the identification to herself. She wanted, let us say, to deal with a certain situation in the way she fancied. And so, being very quick-witted, she deliberately pointed to the *wrong* picture. Thereby keeping her knowledge to herself.'

'But why?'

'Because, as I say, she wanted to play a lone hand.'

'It wouldn't be blackmail? She was an extremely wealthy woman, you know, widow of a North Country manufacturer.'

'Oh no, not blackmail. More likely beneficence. We'll say that she quite liked the person in question, and that she didn't want to give their secret away. But nevertheless she was *curious*. She intended to have a private talk with that person. And whilst doing so, to make up her mind whether or not that person had had anything to do with the death of Mrs McGinty. Something like that.'

'Then that leaves the other three photos in?'

'Precisely. Mrs Upward meant to get in touch with the person in question at the first opportunity. That came when her son and Mrs Oliver went over to the Repertory Theatre at Cullenquay.'

'*And she telephoned to Deirdre Hender-son.* That puts Deirdre Henderson right back in the picture. And her mother!'

Superintendent Spence shook his head sadly at Poirot.

'You do like to make it difficult, don't you, M. Poirot?' he said.

265

21

Mrs Wetherby walked back home from the post office with a gait surprisingly spry in one habitually reported to be an invalid.

Only when she had entered the front door did she once more shuffle feebly into the drawing-room and collapse on the sofa.

The bell was within reach of her hand and she rang it.

Since nothing happened she rang it again, this time keeping her finger on it for some time.

In due course Maude Williams appeared. She was wearing a flowered overall and had a duster in her hand.

'Did you ring, madam?'

'I rang twice. When I ring I expect someone to come at once. I might be dangerously ill.'

'I'm sorry, madam. I was upstairs.'

'I know you were. You were in my room. I heard you overhead. And you were pulling the drawers in and out. I can't think why. It's no part of your job to go prying into my things.'

'I wasn't prying. I was putting some of the

things you left lying about away tidily.'

'Nonsense. All you people snoop. And I won't have it. I'm feeling very faint. Is Miss Deirdre in?'

'She took the dog for a walk.'

'How stupid. She might know I would need her. Bring me an egg beaten up in milk and a little brandy. The brandy is on the sideboard in the dining-room.'

'There are only just the three eggs for breakfast tomorrow.'

'Then someone will have to go without. Hurry, will you? Don't stand there looking at me. And you're wearing far too much make-up. It isn't suitable.'

There was a bark in the hall and Deirdre and her Sealyham came in as Maude went out.

'I heard your voice,' said Deirdre breathlessly. 'What have you been saying to her?'

'Nothing.'

'She looked like thunder.'

'I put her in her place. Impertinent girl.'

'Oh, Mummy darling, must you? It's so difficult to get anyone. And she does cook well.'

'I suppose it's of no importance that she's insolent to *me*! Oh well, I shan't be with you much longer.' Mrs Wetherby rolled up her eyes and took some fluttering breaths. 'I walked too far,' she murmured.

'You oughtn't to have gone out, darling. Why didn't you tell me you were going?'

'I thought some air would do me good. It's so stuffy. It doesn't matter. One doesn't really want to live — not if one's only a trouble to people.'

'You're not a trouble, darling. I'd die without you.'

'You're a good girl — but I can see how I weary you and get on your nerves.'

'You don't — you don't,' said Deirdre passionately.

Mrs Wetherby sighed and let her eyelids fall.

'I — can't talk much,' she murmured. 'I must just lie still.'

'I'll hurry up Maude with the egg nog.'

Deirdre ran out of the room. In her hurry she caught her elbow on a table and a bronze god bumped to the ground.

'So clumsy,' murmured Mrs Wetherby to herself, wincing.

The door opened and Mr Wetherby came in. He stood there for a moment. Mrs Wetherby opened her eyes.

'Oh, it's you, Roger?'

'I wondered what all the noise was in here. It's impossible to read quietly in this house.'

'It was just Deirdre, dear. She came in with the dog.'

Mr Wetherby stooped and picked up the bronze monstrosity from the floor.

'Surely Deirdre's old enough not to knock things down the whole time.'

'She's just rather awkward.'

'Well, it's absurd to be awkward at her age. And can't she keep that dog from barking?'

'I'll speak to her, Roger.'

'If she makes her home here, she must consider our wishes and not behave as though the house belonged to her.'

'Perhaps you'd rather she went away,' murmured Mrs Wetherby. Through half-closed eyes she watched her husband.

'No, of course not. Of course not. Naturally her home is with us. I only ask for a little more good sense and good manners.' He added: 'You've been out, Edith?'

'Yes. I just went down to the post office.'

'No fresh news about poor Mrs Upward?'

'The police still don't know who it was.'

'They seem to be quite hopeless. Any motive? Who gets her money?'

'The son, I suppose.'

'Yes — yes, then it really seems as though it must have been one of these tramps. You should tell this girl she's got to be careful

269

about keeping the front door locked. And only to open it on the chain when it gets near dusk. These men are very daring and brutal nowadays.'

'Nothing seems to have been taken from Mrs Upward's.'

'Odd.'

'Not like Mrs McGinty,' said Mrs Wetherby.

'Mrs McGinty? Oh! the charwoman. What's Mrs McGinty got to do with Mrs Upward?'

'She did work for her, Roger.'

'Don't be silly, Edith.'

Mrs Wetherby closed her eyes again. As Mr Wetherby went out of the room she smiled to herself.

She opened her eyes with a start to find Maude standing over her, holding a glass.

'Your egg nog, madam,' said Maude.

Her voice was loud and clear. It echoed too resonantly in the deadened house.

Mrs Wetherby looked up with a vague feeling of alarm.

How tall and unbending the girl was. She stood over Mrs Wetherby like — 'like a figure of doom,' Mrs Wetherby thought to herself — and then wondered why such extraordinary words had come into her head.

She raised herself on her elbow and took the glass.

'Thank you, Maude,' she said.

Maude turned and went out of the room.

Mrs Wetherby still felt vaguely upset.

22

Hercule Poirot took a hired car back to Broadhinny.

He was tired because he had been thinking. Thinking was always exhausting. And his thinking had not been entirely satisfactory. It was as though a pattern, perfectly visible, was woven into a piece of material and yet, although he was holding the piece of material, he could not see what the pattern was.

But it was all there. That was the point. It was all there. Only it was one of those patterns, self-coloured and subtle, that are not easy to perceive.

A little way out of Kilchester his car encountered the Summerhayes' station wagon coming in the opposite direction. Johnnie was driving and he had a passenger. Poirot hardly noticed them. He was still absorbed in thought.

When he got back to Long Meadows, he went into the drawing-room. He removed a colander full of spinach from the most comfortable chair in the room and sat down. From overhead came the faint drumming of a typewriter. It was Robin Upward, struggling with a play. Three versions he had already torn up, so he told Poirot. Somehow, he couldn't concentrate.

Robin might feel his mother's death quite sincerely, but he remained Robin Upward, chiefly interested in himself.

'Madre,' he said solemnly, 'would have wished me to go on with my work.'

Hercule Poirot had heard many people say much the same thing. It was one of the most convenient assumptions, this knowledge of what the dead would wish. The bereaved had never any doubt about their dear ones' wishes and those wishes usually squared with their own inclinations.

In this case it was probably true. Mrs Upward had had great faith in Robin's work and had been extremely proud of him.

Poirot leaned back and closed his eyes.

He thought of Mrs Upward. He considered what Mrs Upward had really been like. He remembered a phrase that he had once heard used by a police officer.

'We'll take him apart and see what makes him tick.'

What had made Mrs Upward tick?

There was a crash, and Maureen Summer-hayes came in. Her hair was flapping madly.

'I can't think what's happened to Johnnie,' she said. 'He just went down to the post office with those special orders. He ought to have been back hours ago. I want him to fix the henhouse door.'

A true gentleman, Poirot feared, would have gallantly offered to fix the henhouse door himself. Poirot did not. He wanted to go on thinking about two murders and about the character of Mrs Upward.

'And I can't find that Ministry of Agriculture form,' continued Maureen. 'I've looked everywhere.'

'The spinach is on the sofa,' Poirot offered helpfully.

Maureen was not worried about spinach.

'The form came last week,' she mused. 'And I must have put it somewhere. Perhaps it was when I was darning that pullover of Johnnie's.'

She swept over to the bureau and started pulling out the drawers. Most of the contents she swept on to the floor ruthlessly. It was agony to Hercule Poirot to watch her.

Suddenly she uttered a cry of triumph.

'Got it!'

Delightedly she rushed from the room.

Hercule Poirot sighed and resumed meditation.

To arrange, with order and precision —

He frowned. The untidy heap of objects on the floor by the bureau distracted his mind. What a way to look for things!

Order and method. That was the thing. Order and method.

Though he had turned sideways in his chair, he could still see the confusion on the floor. Sewing things, a pile of socks, letters, knitting wool, magazines, sealing wax, photographs, a pullover —

It was insupportable!

Poirot rose, went across to the bureau and with quick deft movements began to return the objects to the open drawers.

The pullover, the socks, the knitting wool. Then, in the next drawer, the sealing wax, the photographs, the letters.

The telephone rang.

The sharpness of the bell made him jump.

He went across to the telephone and lifted the receiver.

''Allo, 'allo, 'allo,' he said.

The voice that spoke to him was the voice of Superintendent Spence.

'Ah! it's you, M. Poirot. Just the man I want.'

Spence's voice was almost unrecognizable.

A very worried man had given place to a confident one.

'Filling me up with a lot of fandangle about the wrong photograph,' he said with reproachful indulgence. 'We've got some new evidence. Girl at the post office in Broadhinny. Major Summerhayes just brought her in. It seems she was standing practically opposite the cottage that night and she saw a woman go in. Some time after eight-thirty and before nine o'clock. And it wasn't Deirdre Henderson. It was a woman with fair hair. That puts us right back where we were — it's definitely between the two of them — Eve Carpenter and Shelagh Rendell. The only question is — which?'

Poirot opened his mouth but did not speak. Carefully, deliberately, he replaced the receiver on the stand.

He stood there staring unseeingly in front of him.

The telephone rang again.

''Allo! 'Allo! 'Allo!'

'Can I speak to M. Poirot, please?'

'Hercule Poirot speaking.'

'Thought so. Maude Williams here. Post office in a quarter of an hour?'

'I will be there.'

He replaced the receiver.

He looked down at his feet. Should he

change his shoes? His feet ached a little. Ah well — no matter.

Resolutely Poirot clapped on his hat and left the house.

On his way down the hill he was hailed by one of Superintendent Spence's men just emerging from Laburnums.

'Morning, M. Poirot.'

Poirot responded politely. He noticed that Sergeant Fletcher was looking excited.

'The Super sent me over to have a thorough check up,' he explained. 'You know — any little thing we might have missed. Never know, do you? We'd been over the desk, of course, but the Super got the idea there might be a secret drawer — must have been reading spy stuff. Well, there wasn't a secret drawer. But after that I got on to the books. Sometimes people slip a letter into a book they're reading. You know?'

Poirot said that he knew. 'And you found something?' he asked politely.

'Not a letter or anything of that sort, no. But I found something interesting — at least I think it's interesting. Look here.'

He unwrapped from a piece of newspaper an old and rather decrepit book.

'In one of the bookshelves it was. Old book, published years ago. But look here.' He opened it and showed the flyleaf. Pencilled across it were the words: *Evelyn Hope*.

'Interesting, don't you think? That's the name, in case you don't remember — '

'The name that Eva Kane took when she left England. I do remember,' said Poirot.

'Looks as though when Mrs McGinty spotted one of those photos here in Broadhinny, it was our Mrs Upward. Makes it kind of complicated, doesn't it?'

'It does,' said Poirot with feeling. 'I can assure you that when you go back to Superintendent Spence with this piece of information he will pull out his hair by the roots — yes, assuredly by the roots.'

'I hope it won't be as bad as that,' said Sergeant Fletcher.

Poirot did not reply. He went on down the hill. He had ceased to think. Nothing anywhere made sense.

He went into the post office. Maude Williams was there looking at knitting patterns. Poirot did not speak to her. He went to the stamp counter. When Maude had made her purchase, Mrs Sweetiman came over to him and he bought some stamps. Maude went out of the shop.

Mrs Sweetiman seemed preoccupied and not talkative. Poirot was able to follow Maude out fairly quickly. He caught her up a short distance along the road and fell into step beside her.

Mrs Sweetiman, looking out of the post office window, exclaimed to herself disapprovingly. 'Those foreigners! All the same, every manjack of 'em. Old enough to be her grandfather, he is!'

II

'*Eh bien*,' said Poirot, 'you have something to tell me?'

'I don't know that it's important. There was somebody trying to get in at the window of Mrs Wetherby's room.'

'When?'

'This morning. *She'd* gone out, and the girl was out with the dog. Old frozen fish was shut up in his study as usual. I'd have been in the kitchen normally — it faces the other way like the study — but actually it seemed a good opportunity to — you understand?'

Poirot nodded.

'So I nipped upstairs and into Her Acidity's bedroom. There was a ladder against the window and a man was fumbling with the window catch. She's had everything locked and barred since the murder. Never a bit of fresh air. When the man saw me he scuttled down and made off. The ladder was the gardener's — he'd been cutting back the ivy and had gone to have his elevenses.'

'Who was the man? Can you describe him?'

'I only got the merest glimpse. By the time I got to the window he was down the ladder and gone, and when I first saw him he was against the sun, so I couldn't see his face.'

'You are sure it *was* a man?'

Maude considered.

'Dressed as a man — an old felt hat on. It *might* have been a woman, of course . . . '

'It is interesting,' said Poirot. 'It is very interesting . . . Nothing else?'

'Not yet. The junk that old woman keeps! Must be dotty! She came in without me hearing this morning and bawled me out for snooping. I shall be murdering her next. If anyone asks to be murdered that woman does. A really nasty bit of goods.'

Poirot murmured softly:

'Evelyn Hope . . . '

'What's that?' She spun round on him.

'So you know that name?'

'Why — yes . . . It's the name Eva Whatsername took when she went to Australia. It — it was in the paper — the *Sunday Comet*.'

'The *Sunday Comet* said many things, but it did not say that. The police found the name

280

written in a book in Mrs Upward's house.'

Maude exclaimed:

'Then it *was* her — and she *didn't* die out there . . . Michael was right.'

'Michael?'

Maude said abruptly:

'I can't stop. I'll be late serving lunch. I've got it all in the oven, but it will be getting dried up.'

She started off at a run. Poirot stood looking after her.

At the post office window, Mrs Sweetiman, her nose glued to the pane, wondered if that old foreigner had been making suggestions of a certain character . . .

III

Back at Long Meadows, Poirot removed his shoes, and put on a pair of bedroom slippers. They were not *chic*, not in his opinion *comme il faut* — but there must be relief.

He sat down on the easy-chair again and began once more to think. He had by now a lot to think about.

There were things he had missed — little things.

The pattern was all there. It only needed cohesion.

Maureen, glass in hand, talking in a dreamy voice — asking a question . . . Mrs Oliver's account of her evening at the Rep. Cecil? Michael? He was almost sure that she had mentioned a Michael — Eva Kane, nursery governess to the Craigs —

Evelyn Hope . . .

Of course! Evelyn Hope!

23

I

Eve Carpenter came into the Summerhayes'
house in the casual way that most people did,
using any door or window that was
convenient.

She was looking for Hercule Poirot and
when she found him she did not beat about
the bush.

'Look here,' she said. 'You're a detective,
and you're supposed to be good. All right, I'll
hire you.'

'Suppose I am not for hire. *Mon Dieu*, I
am not a taxicab!'

'You're a private detective and private
detectives get paid, don't they?'

'It is the custom.'

'Well, that's what I'm saying. I'll pay you.
I'll pay you well.'

'For what? What do you want me to do?'

Eve Carpenter said sharply:

'Protect me against the police. They're
crazy. They seem to think I killed the
Upward woman. And they're nosing round,

asking me all sorts of questions — ferreting out things. I don't like it. It's driving me mental.'

Poirot looked at her. Something of what she said was true. She looked many years older than when he had first seen her a few weeks ago. Circles under her eyes spoke of sleepless nights. There were lines from her mouth to her chin, and her hand, when she lit a cigarette, shook badly.

'You've got to stop it,' she said. 'You've got to.'

'Madame, what can I do?'

'Fend them off somehow or other. Damned cheek! If Guy was a man he'd stop all this. He wouldn't let them persecute me.'

'And — he does nothing?'

She said sullenly:

'I've not told him. He just talks pompously about giving the police all the assistance possible. It's all right for *him*. He was at some ghastly political meeting that night.'

'And you?'

'I was just sitting at home. Listening to the radio actually.'

'But, if you can prove that — '

'How can I prove it? I offered the Crofts a fabulous sum to say they'd been in and out and seen me there — the damned swine refused.'

'That was a very unwise move on your part.'

'I don't see why. It would have settled the business.'

'You have probably convinced your servants that you did commit the murder.'

'Well — I'd paid Croft anyway for — '

'For what?'

'Nothing.'

'Remember — you want my help.'

'Oh! It was nothing that matters. But Croft took the message from her.'

'From Mrs Upward?'

'Yes. Asking me to go down and see her that night.'

'And you say you didn't go?'

'Why should I go? Damned dreary old woman. Why should I go and hold her hand? I never dreamed of going for a moment.'

'When did this message come?'

'When I was out. I don't know exactly when — between five and six, I think. Croft took it.'

'And you gave him money to forget he had taken that message. Why?'

'Don't be idiotic. I didn't want to get mixed up in it all.'

'And then you offer him money to give you an alibi? What do you suppose he and his wife think?'

'Who cares what they think?'

'A jury may care,' said Poirot gravely.

She stared at him.

'You're not serious?'

'I am serious.'

'They'd listen to servants — and not to me?'

Poirot looked at her.

Such crass rudeness and stupidity! Antagonizing the people who might have been helpful. A short-sighted stupid policy. Short-sighted —

Such lovely wide blue eyes.

He said quietly:

'Why don't you wear glasses, madame? You need them.'

'What? Oh, I do sometimes. I did as a child.'

'And you had then a plate for your teeth.'

She stared.

'I did, as a matter of fact. Why all this?'

'The ugly duckling becomes a swan?'

'I was certainly ugly enough.'

'Did your mother think so?'

She said sharply:

'I don't remember my mother. What the hell are we talking about anyway? Will you take on the job?'

'I regret I cannot.'

'Why can't you?'

'Because in this affair I act for James Bentley.'

'James Bentley? Oh, you mean that half-wit who killed the charwoman. What's he got to do with the Upwards?'

'Perhaps — nothing.'

'Well, then! Is it a question of money? How much?'

'That is your great mistake, madame. You think always in terms of money. You have money and you think that only money counts.'

'I haven't always had money,' said Eve Carpenter.

'No,' said Poirot. 'I thought not.' He nodded his head gently. 'That explains a good deal. It excuses some things . . . '

II

Eve Carpenter went out the way she had come, blundering a little in the light as Poirot remembered her doing before.

Poirot said softly to himself: 'Evelyn Hope . . . '

So Mrs Upward had rung up both Deirdre Henderson *and* Evelyn Carpenter. Perhaps she had rung up someone else. Perhaps —

With a crash Maureen came in.

'It's my scissors now. Sorry lunch is late. I've got three pairs and I can't find one of them.'

She rushed over to the bureau and the process with which Poirot was well acquainted was repeated. This time, the objective was attained rather sooner. With a cry of joy, Maureen departed.

Almost automatically, Poirot stepped over and began to replace the things in the drawer. Sealing wax, note-paper, a work basket, photographs —

Photographs . . .

He stood staring at the photograph he held in his hand.

Footsteps rushed back along the passage.

Poirot could move quickly in spite of his age. He had dropped the photograph on the sofa, put a cushion on it, and had himself sat on the cushion, by the time that Maureen re-entered.

'Where the hell've I put a colander full of spinach — '

'But it is there, madame.'

He indicated the colander as it reposed beside him on the sofa.

'So that's where I left it.' She snatched it up. 'Everything's behind today . . . ' Her glance took in Hercule Poirot sitting bolt upright.

'What on earth do you want to sit there for? Even on a cushion, it's the most uncomfortable seat in the room. All the springs are broken.'

'I know, madame. But I am — I am admiring that picture on the wall.'

Maureen glanced up at the oil painting of a naval officer complete with telescope.

'Yes — it's good. About the only good thing in the house. We're not sure that it isn't a Gainsborough.' She sighed. 'Johnnie won't sell it, though. It's his great-great and I think a few more greats, grandfather and he went down with his ship or did something frightfully gallant. Johnnie's terribly proud of it.'

'Yes,' said Poirot gently. 'Yes, he has something to be proud about, your husband!'

III

It was three o'clock when Poirot arrived at Dr Rendell's house.

He had eaten rabbit stew and spinach and hard potatoes and a rather peculiar pudding, not scorched this time. Instead, 'The water got in,' Maureen had explained. He had drunk half a cup of muddy coffee. He did not feel well.

The door was opened by the elderly housekeeper Mrs Scott, and he asked for Mrs Rendell.

She was in the drawing-room with the radio on and started up when he was announced.

He had the same impression of her that he had had the first time he saw her. Wary, on her guard, frightened of him, or frightened of what he represented.

She seemed paler and more shadowy than she had done. He was almost certain that she was thinner.

'I want to ask you a question, madame.'

'A question? Oh? Oh yes?'

'Did Mrs Upward telephone to you on the day of her death?'

She stared at him. She nodded.

'At what time?'

'Mrs Scott took the message. It was about six o'clock, I think.'

'What was the message? To ask you to go there that evening?'

'Yes. She said that Mrs Oliver and Robin were going into Kilchester and she would be all alone as it was Janet's night out. Could I come down and keep her company.'

'Was any time suggested?'

'Nine o'clock or after.'

'And you went?'

'I meant to. I really meant to. But I don't know how it was, I fell fast asleep after dinner that night. It was after ten when I woke up. I thought it was too late.'

'You did not tell the police about Mrs Upward's call?'

Her eyes widened. They had a rather innocent childlike stare.

'Ought I to have done? Since I didn't go, I thought it didn't matter. Perhaps, even, I felt rather guilty. If I'd gone, she might have been alive now.' She caught her breath suddenly. 'Oh, I hope it wasn't like that.'

'Not quite like that,' said Poirot.

He paused and then said:

'*What are you afraid of, madame?*'

She caught her breath sharply.

'Afraid? I'm not afraid.'

'But you are.'

'What nonsense. What — what should I be afraid of?'

Poirot paused for a moment before speaking.

'I thought perhaps you might be afraid of *me* . . . '

She didn't answer. But her eyes widened. Slowly, defiantly, she shook her head.

24

'This way to Bedlam,' said Spence.

'It is not as bad as that,' said Poirot soothingly.

'That's what you say. Every single bit of information that comes in makes things more difficult. Now you tell me that Mrs Upward rang up *three* women. Asked them to come that evening. Why three? Didn't she know herself which of them was Lily Gamboll? Or isn't it a case of Lily Gamboll at all? Take that book with the name of Evelyn Hope in it. It suggests, doesn't it, that Mrs Upward and Eva Kane are one and the same.'

'Which agrees exactly with James Bentley's impression of what Mrs McGinty said to him.'

'I thought he wasn't sure.'

'He was not sure. It would be impossible for James Bentley to be sure of anything. He did not listen properly to what Mrs McGinty was saying. Nevertheless, if James Bentley had an impression that Mrs McGinty was talking about Mrs Upward, it may very well be true. Impressions often are.'

'Our latest information from Australia (it was Australia she went to, by the way, not America) seems to be to the effect that the 'Mrs Hope' in question died out there twenty years ago.'

'I have already been told that,' said Poirot.

'You always know everything, don't you, Poirot?'

Poirot took no notice of this gibe. He said:

'At the one end we have 'Mrs Hope' deceased in Australia — and at the other?'

'At the other end we have Mrs Upward, the widow of a rich North Country manufacturer. She lived with him near Leeds, and had a son. Soon after the son's birth, her husband died. The boy was inclined to be tubercular and since her husband's death she lived mostly abroad.'

'And when does this saga begin?'

'The saga begins four years after Eva Kane left England. Upward met his wife somewhere abroad and brought her home after the marriage.'

'So actually Mrs Upward *could* be Eva Kane. What was her maiden name?'

'Hargraves, I understand. But what's in a name?'

'What indeed. Eva Kane, or Evelyn Hope, may have died in Australia — but she may have arranged a convenient decease and resuscitated herself as Hargraves and made a wealthy match.'

'It's all a long time ago,' said Spence. 'But supposing that it's true. Supposing she kept a picture of herself and supposing that Mrs McGinty saw it — then one can only assume that *she* killed Mrs McGinty.'

'That could be, could it not? Robin Upward was broadcasting that night. Mrs Rendell mentions going to the cottage that evening, remember, and not being able to make herself heard. According to Mrs Sweetiman, Janet Groom told her that Mrs Upward was not really as crippled as she made out.'

'That's all very well, Poirot, but the fact remains that *she herself* was killed — after recognizing a photograph. Now you want to make out that the two deaths are not connected.'

'No, no. I do not say that. They are connected all right.'

'I give it up.'

'Evelyn Hope. There is the key to the problem.'

'Evelyn Carpenter? Is that your idea? *Not* Lily Gamboll — but Eva Kane's daughter!

But surely she wouldn't kill her own mother.'

'No, no. This is not matricide.'

'What an irritating devil you are, Poirot. You'll be saying next that Eva Kane and Lily Gamboll, and Janice Courtland *and* Vera Blake are *all* living in Broadhinny. All four suspects.'

'We have more than four. Eva Kane was the Craigs' nursery governess, remember.'

'What's that got to do with it?'

'Where there is a nursery governess, there must be children — or at least a child. What happened to the Craig children?'

'There was a girl and a boy, I believe. Some relative took them.'

'So there are two more people to take into account. Two people who might have kept a photograph for the third reason I mentioned — revenge.'

'I don't believe it,' said Spence.

Poirot sighed.

'It has to be considered, all the same. I think I know the truth — though there is one fact that baffles me utterly.'

'I'm glad something baffles you,' said Spence.

'Confirm one thing for me, *mon cher* Spence. Eva Kane left the country before Craig's execution, that is right?'

'Quite right.'

'And she was, at that time, expecting a child?'

'Quite right.'

'*Bon Dieu*, how stupid I have been,' said Hercule Poirot. 'The whole thing is simple, is it not?'

It was after that remark that there was very nearly a third murder — the murder of Hercule Poirot by Superintendent Spence in Kilchester Police Headquarters.

II

'I want,' said Hercule Poirot, 'a personal call. To Mrs Ariadne Oliver.'

A personal call to Mrs Oliver was not achieved without difficulties. Mrs Oliver was working and could not be disturbed. Poirot, however, disregarded all denials. Presently he heard the authoress's voice.

It was cross and rather breathless.

'Well, what is it?' said Mrs Oliver. 'Have you got to ring me up just now? I've thought of a most wonderful idea for a murder in a draper's shop. You know, the old-fashioned kind that sells combinations and funny vests with long sleeves.'

'I do not know,' said Poirot. 'And anyway

what I have to say to you is far more important.'

'It couldn't be,' said Mrs Oliver. 'Not to *me*, I mean. Unless I get a rough sketch of my idea jotted down, it will *go!*'

Hercule Poirot paid no attention to this creative agony. He asked sharp imperative questions to which Mrs Oliver replied somewhat vaguely.

'Yes — yes — it's a little Repertory Theatre — I don't know its name . . . Well, one of them was Cecil Something, and the one I was talking to was Michael.'

'Admirable. That is all I need to know.'

'But why Cecil and Michael?'

'Return to the combinations and the long-sleeved vests, madame.'

'I can't think why you don't arrest Dr Rendell,' said Mrs Oliver. 'I would, if I were the Head of Scotland Yard.'

'Very possibly. I wish you luck with the murder in the draper's shop.'

'The whole idea has gone now,' said Mrs Oliver. 'You've ruined it.'

Poirot apologized handsomely.

He put down the receiver and smiled at Spence.

'We go now — or at least I will go — to interview a young actor whose Christian name is Michael and who plays the less important parts in the Cullenquay Repertory Theatre. I pray only that he is the right Michael.'

'Why on earth — '

Poirot dexterously averted the rising wrath of Superintendent Spence.

'Do you know, *cher ami,* what is a *secret de Polichinelle?*'

'Is this a French lesson?' demanded the superintendent wrathfully.

'A *secret de Polichinelle* is a secret that everyone can know. For this reason the people who do not know it never hear about it — for if everyone thinks you know a thing, nobody tells you.'

'How I manage to keep my hands off you I don't know,' said Superintendent Spence.

25

The inquest was over — a verdict had been returned of murder by a person or persons unknown.

After the inquest, at the invitation of Hercule Poirot, those who had attended it came to Long Meadows,

Working diligently, Poirot had induced some semblance of order in the long drawing-room. Chairs had been arranged in a neat semi-circle, Maureen's dogs had been excluded with difficulty, and Hercule Poirot, a self-appointed lecturer, took up his position at the end of the room and initiated proceedings with a slightly self-conscious clearing of the throat.

'Messieurs et Mesdames — '

He paused. His next words were unexpected and seemed almost farcical.

'Mrs McGinty's dead. How did she die?
Down on her knees just like I.
Mrs McGinty's dead. How did she die?
Holding her hand out just like I.
Mrs McGinty's dead. How did she die?
Like this . . . '

Seeing their expressions, he went on:

'No, I am not mad. Because I repeat to you the childish rhyme of a childish game, it does not mean that I am in my second childhood. Some of you may have played that game as children. Mrs Upward had played it. Indeed she repeated it to me — with a difference. She said: '*Mrs McGinty's dead. How did she die? Sticking her neck out just like I.*' That is what she said — and that is what she did. She stuck her neck out — and so she also, like Mrs McGinty, died . . .

'For our purpose we must go back to the beginning — to Mrs McGinty — down on her knees scrubbing other people's houses, Mrs McGinty was killed, and a man, James Bentley, was arrested, tried and convicted. For certain reasons, Superintendent Spence, the officer in charge of the case, was not convinced of Bentley's guilt, strong though the evidence was. I agreed with him. I came down here to answer a question. 'How did Mrs McGinty die? *Why* did she die?'

'I will not make you the long and complicated histories. I will say only that as simple a thing as a bottle of ink gave me a clue. In the *Sunday Comet*, read by Mrs McGinty on the Sunday before her death, four photographs were published. You know all about those photographs by now, so I will only say that Mrs McGinty recognized one of those photographs as a photograph she had seen in one of the houses where she worked.

'She spoke of this to James Bentley though he attached no importance to the matter at the time, nor indeed afterwards. Actually he barely listened. But he had the impression that Mrs McGinty had seen the photograph in Mrs Upward's house and that when she referred to a woman who need not be so proud if all was known, she was referring to Mrs Upward. We cannot depend on that statement of his, but she certainly used that phrase about pride and there is no doubt that Mrs Upward *was* a proud and imperious woman.

'As you all know — some of you were present and the others will have heard — I produced those four photographs at Mrs Upward's house. I caught a flicker of surprise and recognition in Mrs Upward's expression and taxed her with it. She had to admit it. She said that she 'had seen one of the photographs somewhere but she couldn't remember where'. When asked which photograph, she pointed to a photograph of the child Lily Gamboll. But that, let me tell you, *was not the truth.* For reasons of her own, Mrs Upward wanted to keep her recognition to herself. She pointed to the wrong photograph to put me off.

'But one person was not deceived — the *murderer*. One person *knew* which photograph Mrs Upward had recognized. And here I will not beat to and fro about the bush — the photograph in question was that of Eva Kane — a woman who was accomplice, victim or possibly leading spirit in the famous Craig Murder Case.

'On the next evening Mrs Upward was killed. She was killed for the same reason that Mrs McGinty was killed. Mrs McGinty stuck her hand out, Mrs Upward stuck her neck out — the result was the same.

'Now before Mrs Upward died, three women received telephone calls. Mrs Carpenter, Mrs Rendell, and Miss Henderson. All three calls were a message from Mrs Upward asking the person in question to come and see her that evening. It was her servant's night out and her son and Mrs Oliver were going into Cullenquay. It would seem, therefore, that she wanted a private conversation with each of these three women.

'Now why *three* women? Did Mrs Upward know *where* she had seen the photograph of Eva Kane? Or did she know she had seen it but could not remember where? Had these three women anything in common? Nothing, it would seem, but their *age*. They were all, roughly, in the neighbourhood of thirty.

'You have, perhaps, read the article in the *Sunday Comet*. There is a truly sentimental picture in it of Eva Kane's daughter in years to come. The women asked by Mrs Upward to come and see her were all of the right age to be Eva Kane's daughter.

'So it would seem that living in Broadhinny was a young woman who was the daughter of the celebrated murderer Craig and of his mistress Eva Kane, and it would also seem that that young woman would go to any lengths to prevent that fact being known. Would go, indeed, to the length of twice committing murder. For when Mrs Upward was found dead, there were two coffee cups on the table, both used, and on the visitor's cup faint traces of lipstick.

'Now let us go back to the three women who received telephone messages. Mrs Carpenter got the message but says she did not go to Laburnums that night. Mrs Rendell meant to go, but fell asleep in her chair. Miss Henderson *did* go to Laburnums but the house was dark and she could not make anyone hear and she came away again.

'That is the story these three woman tell — but there is conflicting evidence. There is that second coffee cup with lipstick on it, and an outside witness, the girl Edna, states positively that she saw a fair-haired woman go *in* to the house. There is also the evidence of scent — an expensive and exotic scent which Mrs Carpenter uses alone of those concerned.'

There was an interruption. Eve Carpenter cried out:

'It's a lie. It's a wicked cruel lie. It wasn't me! I never went there! I never went near the place. Guy, can't you do something about these lies?'

Guy Carpenter was white with anger.

'Let me inform you, M. Poirot, that there is a law of slander and all these people present are witnesses.'

'Is it slander to say that your wife uses a certain scent — and also, let me tell you, a certain lipstick?'

'It's ridiculous,' cried Eve. 'Absolutely ridiculous! *Anyone* could go splashing my scent about.'

Unexpectedly Poirot beamed on her.

'*Mais oui*, exactly! Anyone could. An obvious, not very subtle thing to do. Clumsy and crude. So clumsy that, as far as I was concerned, it defeated its object. It did more. It gave me, as the phrase goes, ideas. Yes, it gave me ideas.

'Scent — and traces of lipstick on a cup. But it is so easy to remove lipstick from a cup

— I assure you every trace can be wiped off quite easily. Or the cups themselves could be removed and washed. Why not? There was no one in the house. But that was not done. I asked myself why? And the answer seemed to be a deliberate stress on femininity, an underlining of the fact that it was a *woman's* murder. I reflected on the telephone calls to those three women — all of them had been *messages*. In no case had the recipient herself spoken to Mrs Upward. So perhaps it was *not* Mrs Upward who had telephoned. It was someone who was anxious to involve a *woman* — *any* woman — in the crime. Again I asked why? And there can only be one answer — that it was not a woman who killed Mrs Upward — but a *man*.'

He looked round on his audience. They were all very still. Only two people responded.

Eve Carpenter said with a sigh: 'Now you're talking sense!'

Mrs Oliver, nodding her head vigorously, said: 'Of course.'

'So I have arrived at this point — a *man* killed Mrs Upward and a *man* killed Mrs McGinty! What man? The reason for the murder must still be the same — it all hinges on a photograph. In whose possession was that photograph? That is the first question.

And why was it kept?

'Well, that is perhaps not so difficult. Say that it was kept originally for sentimental reasons. Once Mrs McGinty is — removed, the photograph need not be destroyed. But after the second murder, it is different. This time the photograph has definitely been connected with the murder. The photograph is now a dangerous thing to keep. Therefore you will all agree, it is sure to be destroyed.'

He looked round at the heads that nodded agreement.

'But, for all that, the photograph was *not* destroyed! No, it was not destroyed! I know that — because I found it. I found it a few days ago. I found it in this house. In the drawer of the bureau that you see standing against the wall. I have it here.'

He held out the faded photograph of a simpering girl with roses.

'Yes,' said Poirot. 'It is Eva Kane. And on the back of it are written two words in pencil. Shall I tell you what they are? '*My mother*' . . . '

His eyes, grave and accusing, rested on Maureen Summerhayes. She pushed back the hair from her face and stared at him with wide bewildered eyes.

'I don't understand. I never — '

'No, Mrs Summerhayes, you do not

306

understand. There can be only two reasons for keeping this photograph after the second murder. The first of them is an innocent sentimentality. You had no feeling of guilt and so you could keep the photograph. You told us yourself, at Mrs Carpenter's house one day, that you were an adopted child. I doubt whether you have ever known what your real mother's name was. But somebody else knew. Somebody who has all the pride of family — a pride that makes him cling to his ancestral home, a pride in his ancestors and his lineage. That man would rather die than have the world — and his children — know that Maureen Summerhayes is the daughter of the murderer Craig and of Eva Kane. That man, I have said, would rather die. But that would not help, would it? So instead let us say that we have here a man who is prepared to kill.'

Johnnie Summerhayes got up from his seat. His voice, when he spoke, was quiet, almost friendly.

'Rather a lot of nonsense you're talkin', aren't you? Enjoying yourself spouting out a lot of theories? Theories, that's all they are! Saying things about my wife — '

His anger broke suddenly in a furious tide. 'You damned filthy swine — '

The swiftness of his rush across the floor

took the room unawares. Poirot skipped back nimbly and Superintendent Spence was suddenly between Poirot and Summerhayes.

'Now, now, Major Summerhayes, take it easy — take it easy — '

Summerhayes recovered himself, shrugged, said:

'Sorry. Ridiculous really! After all — any-one can stick a photograph in a drawer.'

'Precisely,' said Poirot. 'And the interesting thing about this photograph is that it has no fingerprints on it.'

He paused, then nodded his head gently.

'But it should have had,' he said. 'If Mrs Summerhayes kept it, she would have kept it innocently, and so her fingerprints *should* have been on it.'

Maureen exclaimed:

'I think you're mad. I've never seen that photograph in my life — except at Mrs Upward's that day.'

'It is fortunate for you,' said Poirot, 'that I know that you are speaking the truth. The photograph was put into that drawer *only a few minutes before I found it there.* Twice that morning the contents of that drawer were tumbled on to the ground, twice I replaced them; the first time the photograph was *not* in the drawer, the second time it *was*. It had been placed there during that interval — *and*

I know by whom.'

A new note crept into his voice. He was no longer a ridiculous little man with an absurd moustache and dyed hair, he was a hunter very close to his quarry.

'The crimes were committed by a *man* — they were committed for the simplest of all reasons — for money. In Mrs Upward's house there was a book found and on the flyleaf of that book is written *Evelyn Hope*. Hope was the name Eva Kane took when she left England. If her real name was Evelyn then in all probability she gave the name of Evelyn to her child when it was born. *But Evelyn is a man's name as well as a woman's.* Why had we assumed that Eva Kane's child was a girl? Roughly because the *Sunday Comet* said so! But actually the *Sunday Comet* had not said so in so many words, it had assumed it because of a romantic interview with Eva Kane. But Eva Kane left England *before* her child was born — so nobody could say what the sex of the child would be.

'That is where I let myself be misled. By the romantic inaccuracy of the Press.

'Evelyn Hope, Eva Kane's *son*, comes to England. He is talented and he attracts the attention of a very rich woman who knows nothing about his origin — only the romantic story he chooses to tell her. (A very pretty little story it was — all about a tragic young ballerina dying of tuberculosis in Paris!)

'She is a lonely woman who has recently lost her own son. The talented young playwright takes her name by deed poll.

'*But your real name is Evelyn Hope, isn't it, Mr Upward?*'

Robin Upward cried out shrilly:

'Of course it isn't! I don't know what you're talking about.'

'You really cannot hope to deny it. There are people who know you under that name. The name Evelyn Hope, written in the book, is in your handwriting — the same handwriting as the words 'my mother' on the back of this photograph. Mrs McGinty saw the photograph and the writing on it when she was tidying your things away. She spoke to you about it after reading the *Sunday Comet*. Mrs McGinty assumed that it was a photograph of *Mrs Upward* when young, since she had no idea Mrs Upward was not your real mother. But you knew that if once she mentioned the matter so that it came to Mrs Upward's ears, it would be the end. Mrs Upward had quite fanatical views on the subject of heredity. She would not tolerate for a moment an adopted son who was the son of a famous murderer. Nor would she forgive your lies on the subject.

'So Mrs McGinty had at all costs to be silenced. You promised her a little present, perhaps, for being discreet. You called on her the next evening on your way to broadcast — and you killed her! *Like this* . . . '

With a sudden movement, Poirot seized the sugar hammer from the shelf and whirled it round and down as though to bring it crashing down on Robin's head.

So menacing was the gesture that several of the circle cried out.

Robin Upward screamed. A high terrified scream.

He yelled: 'Don't . . . don't . . . It was an accident. I swear it was an accident. I didn't mean to kill her. I lost my head. I swear I did.'

'You washed off the blood and put the sugar hammer back in this room where you had found it. But there are new scientific methods of determining blood stains — and of bringing up latent fingerprints.'

'I tell you I never meant to kill her . . . It was all a mistake . . . And anyway it isn't my fault . . . I'm not responsible. It's in my blood. I can't help it. You can't hang me for something that isn't my fault . . . '

Under his breath Spence muttered: 'Can't we? You see if we don't!'

Aloud he spoke in a grave official voice:

'I must warn you, Mr Upward, that anything you say . . . '

26

'I really don't see, M. Poirot, how ever you came to suspect Robin Upward.'

Poirot looked complacently at the faces turned towards him.

He always enjoyed explanations.

'I ought to have suspected him much sooner. The clue, such a simple clue, was the sentence uttered by Mrs Summerhayes at the cocktail party that day. She said to Robin Upward: 'I don't like being adopted, do you?' Those were the revealing two words. *Do you?* They meant — they could only mean — that Mrs Upward was not Robin's own mother.

'Mrs Upward was morbidly anxious herself that no one should know that Robin was not her own son. She had probably heard too many ribald comments on brilliant young men who live with and upon elderly women. And very few people did know — only the small theatrical *coterie* where she had first come across Robin. She had few intimate friends in this country, having lived abroad so long, and she chose in any case to come and settle down here far away from her own Yorkshire. Even when she met friends of the old days, she did not enlighten them when they assumed that this Robin was the same Robin they had known as a little boy.

'But from the very first something had struck me as not quite natural in the household at Laburnums. Robin's attitude to Mrs Upward was not that of either a spoiled child, or of a devoted son. It was the attitude of a protégé to a *patron*. The rather fanciful title of Madre had a theatrical touch. And Mrs Upward, though she was clearly very fond of Robin, nevertheless unconsciously treated him as a prized possession that she had bought and paid for.

'So there is Robin Upward, comfortably established, with 'Madre's' purse to back his ventures, and then into his assured world comes Mrs McGinty who has recognized the photograph that he keeps in a drawer — the photograph with 'my mother' written on the back of it. His mother, who he has told Mrs Upward was a talented young ballet dancer who died of tuberculosis! Mrs McGinty, of course, thinks that the photograph is of Mrs Upward when young, since she assumes as a matter of course that Mrs Upward is Robin's own mother. I do not think that actual blackmail ever entered Mrs McGinty's mind, but she did hope, perhaps, for a 'nice little present', as a reward for holding her tongue about a piece of bygone gossip which would not have been pleasant for a 'proud' woman like Mrs Upward.

'But Robin Upward was taking no chances. He purloins the sugar hammer, laughingly referred to as a perfect weapon for murder by Mrs Summerhayes, and on the following evening, he stops at Mrs McGinty's cottage on his way to broadcast. She takes him into the parlour, quite unsuspicious, and he kills her. He knows where she keeps her savings — everyone in Broadhinny seems to know — and he fakes a burglary, hiding the money outside the house. Bentley is suspected and arrested. Everything is now safe for clever Robin Upward.

'But then, suddenly, I produce four photographs, and Mrs Upward recognizes the one of Eva Kane as being identical with a photograph of Robin's ballerina mother! She needs a little time to think things out. Murder is involved. Can it be possible that Robin — ? No, she refuses to believe it.

'What action she would have taken in the end we do not know. But Robin was taking no chances. He plans the whole *mise en scène*. The visit to the Rep on Janet's night out, the telephone calls, the coffee cup carefully smeared with lipstick taken from Eve Carpenter's bag, he even buys a bottle of her distinctive perfume. The whole thing was a theatrical scene setting with prepared props. Whilst Mrs Oliver waited in the car, Robin ran back twice into the house. The murder was a matter of seconds. After that there was only the swift distribution of the 'props'. And with Mrs Upward dead, he inherited a large fortune by the terms of her will, and no suspicion could attach to him since it would seem quite certain that a *woman* had committed the crime. With three women visiting the cottage that night, one of them was almost sure to be suspected. And that, indeed, was so.

'But Robin, like all criminals, was careless and over confident. Not only was there a book in the cottage with his original name scribbled in it, but he also kept, for purposes of his own, the fatal photograph. It would have been much safer for him if he had destroyed it, but he clung to the belief that he could use it to incriminate someone else at the right moment.

'He probably thought then of Mrs Summerhayes. That may be the reason he moved out of the cottage and into Long Meadows. After all, the sugar hammer was hers, and Mrs Summerhayes was, he knew, an adopted child and might find it hard to prove she was not Eva Kane's daughter.

'However, when Deirdre Henderson admitted having been on the scene of the crime, he conceived the idea of planting the photograph amongst *her* possessions. He tried to do so, using a ladder that the gardener had left against the window. But Mrs Wetherby was nervous and had insisted on all the windows being kept locked, so Robin did not succeed in his purpose. He came straight back here and put the photograph in a drawer which, unfortunately for him, I had searched only a short time before.

'I knew, therefore, that the photograph had been planted, and I knew by whom — by the only person in the house — that person who was typing industriously over my head.

'Since the name Evelyn Hope had been written on the flyleaf of the book from the cottage, Evelyn Hope must be either Mrs Upward — or Robin Upward . . .

'The name Evelyn had led me astray — I had connected it with Mrs Carpenter since her name was Eve. *But Evelyn was a man's name as well as a woman's.*

'I remembered the conversation Mrs Oliver had told me about at the Little Rep in Cullenquay. The young actor who had been talking to her was the person I wanted to confirm my theory — the theory that Robin was not Mrs Upward's own son. For by the way he had talked, it seemed clear that he knew the real facts. And his story of Mrs Upward's swift retribution on a young man who had deceived her as to his origins was suggestive.

'The truth is that I ought to have seen the whole thing very much sooner. I was handicapped by a serious error. I believed that I had been deliberately pushed with the intention of sending me on to a railway line — and that the person who had done so was the murderer of Mrs McGinty. Now Robin Upward was practically the only person in Broadhinny who could *not* have been at Kilchester station at that time.'

There was a sudden chuckle from Johnnie Summerhayes.

'Probably some old woman with a basket. They do shove.'

Poirot said:

'Actually, Robin Upward was far too conceited to fear me at all. It is a characteristic of murderers. Fortunately, perhaps. For in this case there was very little evidence.'

Mrs Oliver stirred.

'Do you mean to say,' she demanded incredulously, 'that Robin murdered his mother whilst I sat outside in the car, and that I hadn't the least idea of it? There wouldn't have been time!'

'Oh yes, there would. People's ideas of time are usually ludicrously wrong. Just notice some time how swiftly a stage can be reset. In this case it was mostly a matter of props.'

'Good theatre,' murmured Mrs Oliver mechanically.

'Yes, it was pre-eminently a theatrical murder. All very much contrived.'

'And I sat there in the car — and hadn't the least idea!'

'I am afraid,' murmured Poirot, 'that your woman's intuition was taking a day off.'

27

'I'm not going back to Breather & Scuttle,' said Maude Williams. 'They're a lousy firm anyway.'

'And they have served their purpose.'

'What do you mean by that, M. Poirot?'

'Why did you come to this part of the world?'

'I suppose being Mr Knowall, you think you know?'

'I have a little idea.'

'And what is this famous idea.'

Poirot was looking meditatively at Maude's hair.

'I have been very discreet,' he said. 'It has been assumed that the woman who went into Mrs Upward's house, the fair-haired woman that Edna saw, was Mrs Carpenter, and that she has denied being there simply out of fright. Since it was Robin Upward who killed Mrs Upward, her presence has no more significance than that of Miss Henderson. But all the same I do not think she *was* there. I think Miss Williams, that the woman Edna saw was *you*.'

'Why me?'

Her voice was hard.

Poirot countered with another question.

'Why were you so interested in Broad-hinny? Why, when you went over there, did you ask Robin Upward for an autograph — you are not the autograph-hunting type. What did you know about the Upwards? Why did you come to this part of the world in the first place? How did you know that Eva Kane died in Australia and the name she took when she left England?'

'Good at guessing, aren't you? Well, I've nothing to hide, not really.'

She opened her handbag. From a worn notecase she pulled out a small newspaper cutting frayed with age. It showed the face that Poirot by now knew so well, the simpering face of Eva Kane.

Written across it were the words, *She killed my mother.*

Poirot handed it back to her.

'Yes, I thought so. Your real name is Craig?'

Maude nodded.

'I was brought up by some cousins — very decent they were. But I was old enough when it all happened not to forget. I used to think about it a good deal. About *her.* She was a nasty bit of goods all right — children know! My father was just — weak. And besotted by her. But he took the rap. For something, I've

321

always believed, that *she* did. Oh yes, I know he's an accessory after the fact — but it's not quite the same thing, is it? I always meant to find out what had become of *her*. When I was grown up, I got detectives on to it. They traced her to Australia and finally reported that she was dead. She'd left a son — Evelyn Hope he called himself.

'Well, that seemed to close the account. But then I got pally with a young actor chap. He mentioned someone called Evelyn Hope who'd come from Australia, but who now called himself Robin Upward and who wrote plays. I was interested. One night Robin Upward was pointed out to me — and he was with his *mother*. So I thought that, after all, Eva Kane *wasn't* dead. Instead, she was queening it about with a packet of money.

'I got myself a job down here. I was curious — and a bit more than curious. All right, I'll admit it, I thought I'd like to get even with her in some way . . . When you brought up all this business about James Bentley, I jumped to the conclusion that it was Mrs Upward who'd killed Mrs McGinty. Eva Kane up to her tricks again. I happened to hear from Michael West that Robin Upward and Mrs Oliver were coming over to this show at the Cullenquay Rep. I decided to go to Broadhinny and beard the woman. I meant

— I don't quite know what I meant. I'm telling you everything — I took a little pistol I had in the war with me. To frighten her? Or more? Honestly, I don't know . . .

'Well, I got there. There was no sound in the house. The door was unlocked. I went in. You know how I found her. Sitting there dead, her face all purple and swollen. All the things I'd been thinking seemed silly and melodramatic. I knew that I'd never, really, want to kill anyone when it came to it . . . But I did realize that it might be awkward to explain what I'd been doing in the house. It was a cold night and I'd got gloves on, so I knew I hadn't left any fingerprints, and I didn't think for a moment anyone had seen me. That's all.' She paused and added abruptly: 'What are you going to do about it?'

'Nothing,' said Hercule Poirot. 'I wish you good luck in life, that is all.'

Epilogue

Hercule Poirot and Superintendent Spence were celebrating at the *La Vieille Grand'mère*.

As coffee was served Spence leaned back in his chair and gave a deep sigh of repletion.

'Not at all bad grub here,' he said approvingly. 'A bit Frenchified, perhaps, but after all where *can* you get a decent steak and chips nowadays?'

'I had been dining here on the evening you first came to me,' said Poirot reminiscently.

'Ah, a lot of water under the bridge since then. I've got to hand it to you, M. Poirot. You did the trick all right.' A slight smile creased his wooden countenance. 'Lucky that young man didn't realize how very little evidence we'd really got. Why, a clever counsel would have made mincemeat of it! But he lost his head completely, and gave the show away. Spilt the beans and incriminated himself up to the hilt. Lucky for us!'

'It was not entirely luck,' said Poirot reprovingly. 'I played him, as you play the big fish! He thinks I take the evidence against Mrs Summerhayes seriously — when it is not so, he suffers the reaction and goes to pieces.

And besides, he is a coward. I whirl the sugar hammer and he thinks I mean to hit him. Acute fear always produces the truth.'

'Lucky you didn't suffer from Major Summerhayes' reaction,' said Spence with a grin. 'Got a temper, he has, *and* quick on his feet. I only got between you just in time. Has he forgiven you yet?'

'Oh yes, we are the firmest friends. And I have given Mrs Summerhayes a cookery book and I have also taught her personally how to make an omelette. *Bon Dieu*, what I suffered in that house!'

He closed his eyes.

'Complicated business, the whole thing,' ruminated Spence, uninterested in Poirot's agonized memories. 'Just shows how true the old saying is that everyone's got something to hide. Mrs Carpenter, now, had a narrow squeak of being arrested for murder. If ever a woman acted guilty, she did, and all for what?'

'*Eh bien*, what?' asked Poirot curiously.

'Just the usual business of a rather unsavoury past. She had been a taxi dancer — and a bright girl with plenty of men friends! She wasn't a war widow when she came and settled down in Broadhinny. Only what they call nowadays an 'unofficial wife'. Well, of course all that wouldn't do for a stuffed shirt like Guy Carpenter, so she'd spun him a very different sort of tale. And she was frantic lest the whole thing would come out once we started poking round into people's origins.'

He sipped his coffee, and then gave a low chuckle.

'Then take the Wetherbys. Sinister sort of house. Hate and malice. Awkward frustrated sort of girl. And what's behind that? Nothing sinister. Just money! Plain £.s.d.'

'As simple as that!'

'The girl has the money — quite a lot of it. Left her by an aunt. So mother keeps tight hold of her in case she should want to marry. And stepfather loathes her because *she* has the dibs and pays the bills. I gather he himself has been a failure at anything he's tried. A mean cuss — and as for Mrs W., she's pure poison dissolved in sugar.'

'I agree with you.' Poirot nodded his head in a satisfied fashion. 'It is fortunate that the girl has money. It makes her marriage to James Bentley much more easy to arrange.'

Superintendent Spence looked surprised.

'Going to marry James Bentley? Deirdre Henderson? Who says so?'

'I say so,' said Poirot. 'I occupy myself with the affair. I have, now that our little problem is over, too much time on my hands. I shall employ myself in forwarding this marriage. As yet, the two concerned have no idea of such a thing. But they are attracted. Left to themselves, nothing would happen — but they have to reckon with Hercule Poirot. You will see! The affair will march.'

Spence grinned.

'Don't mind sticking your fingers in other people's pies, do you?'

'*Mon cher*, that does not come well from you,' said Poirot reproachfully.

'Well, you've got me there. All the same, James Bentley is a poor stick.'

'Certainly he is a poor stick! At the moment he is positively aggrieved because he is not going to be hanged.'

'He ought to be down on his knees with gratitude to you,' said Spence.

'Say, rather, to you. But apparently he does not think so.'

'Queer cuss.'

'As you say, and yet at least two women have been prepared to take an interest in him. Nature is very unexpected.'

'I thought it was Maude Williams you were going to pair off with him.'

'He shall make his choice,' said Poirot. 'He shall — how do you say it? — award the apple. But I think that it is Deirdre Henderson that he will choose. Maude

Williams has too much energy and vitality. With her he would retire even farther into his shell.'

'Can't think why either of them should want him!'

'The ways of nature are indeed inscrutable.'

'All the same, you'll have your work cut out. First bringing him up to the scratch — and then prising the girl loose from poison puss mother — she'll fight you tooth and claw!'

'Success is on the side of the big battalions.'

'On the side of the big moustaches, I suppose you mean.'

Spence roared. Poirot stroked his moustache complacently and suggested a brandy.

'I don't mind if I do, M. Poirot.'

Poirot gave the order.

'Ah,' said Spence, 'I knew there was something else I had to tell you. You remember the Rendells?'

'Naturally.'

'Well, when we were checking up on him, something rather odd came to light. It seems that when his first wife died in Leeds where his practice was at that time, the police there got some rather nasty anonymous letters about him. Saying, in effect, that he'd poisoned her. Of course people do say that sort of thing. She'd been attended by an outside doctor, reputable man, and he seemed to think her death was quite above board. There was nothing to go upon except the fact that they'd mutually insured their lives in each other's favour, and people do do that . . . Nothing for us to go upon, as I say, and yet — I wonder? What do *you* think?'

Poirot remembered Mrs Rendell's frightened air. Her mention of anonymous letters, and her insistence that she did not believe anything they said. He remembered, too, her certainty that his inquiry about Mrs McGinty was only a pretext.

He said, 'I should imagine that it was not only the police who got anonymous letters.'

'Sent them to her, too?'

'I think so. When I appeared in Broadhinny, she thought I was on her husband's track, and that the McGinty business was a pretext. Yes — and he thought so, too . . . That explains it! It was Dr Rendell who tried to push me under the train that night!'

'Think he'll have a shot at doing this wife in, too?'

'I think she would be wise not to insure her life in his favour,' said Poirot drily. 'But if he believes we have an eye on him he will probably be prudent.'

'We'll do what we can. We'll keep an eye on our genial doctor, and make it clear we're doing so.'

Poirot raised his brandy glass.

'To Mrs Oliver,' he said.

'What put her into your head suddenly?'

'Woman's intuition,' said Poirot.

There was silence for a moment, then Spence said slowly: 'Robin Upward is coming up for trial next week. You know, Poirot, I can't help feeling doubtful — '

Poirot interrupted him with horror.

'*Mon Dieu!* You are not now doubtful about Robin Upward's guilt, are you? Do not say you want to start over again.'

Superintendent Spence grinned reassuringly.

'Good Lord, no. *He's* a murderer all right!' He added: 'Cocky enough for anything!'

The Agatha Christie Collection
Published by The House of Ulverscroft:

THE MAN IN THE BROWN SUIT
THE SECRET OF CHIMNEYS
THE SEVEN DIALS MYSTERY
THE MYSTERIOUS MR QUIN
THE SITTAFORD MYSTERY
THE HOUND OF DEATH
THE LISTERDALE MYSTERY
WHY DIDN'T THEY ASK EVANS?
PARKER PYNE INVESTIGATES
MURDER IS EASY
AND THEN THERE WERE NONE
TOWARDS ZERO
DEATH COMES AS THE END
SPARKLING CYANIDE
CROOKED HOUSE
THEY CAME TO BAGHDAD
DESTINATION UNKNOWN
ORDEAL BY INNOCENCE
THE PALE HORSE
ENDLESS NIGHT
PASSENGER TO FRANKFURT
PROBLEM AT POLLENSA BAY
WHILE THE LIGHT LASTS

MISS MARPLE
THE MURDER AT THE VICARAGE
THE THIRTEEN PROBLEMS
THE BODY IN THE LIBRARY
THE MOVING FINGER

We do hope that you have enjoyed reading this large print book.

Did you know that all of our titles are available for purchase?

We publish a wide range of high quality large print books including:
Romances, Mysteries, Classics
General Fiction
Non Fiction and Westerns

Special interest titles available in large print are:
The Little Oxford Dictionary
Music Book
Song Book
Hymn Book
Service Book

Also available from us courtesy of Oxford University Press:
Young Readers' Dictionary
(large print edition)
Young Readers' Thesaurus
(large print edition)

For further information or a free brochure, please contact us at:
Ulverscroft Large Print Books Ltd.,
The Green, Bradgate Road, Anstey,
Leicester, LE7 7FU, England.
Tel: (00 44) 0116 236 4325
Fax: (00 44) 0116 234 0205